"Champions keep playing until they get it right."
-Billie Jean King

Aggressive Publishing, Inc.

Editing, design and distribution by Bublish

ISBN: 978-0-9965195-4-0 (paperback)
ISBN: 978-0-9965195-5-7 (eBook)

TANGLED VERDICT

Katherine Smith Dedrick

CHAPTER

1

PEEKING AROUND THE heavy curtain and standing just out of view, Victoria watched as Johnnie egged the crowd into an excited frenzy. Her heart began to pound, the natural performer in her knowing it was almost time. Feeling her phone vibrate in her pocket, she took it out to read the text, smiling as she did so. *Go get 'em, V!* Armond was always there for her.

"And with that"—the stomping, clapping, and shouting increased—"let's welcome the next senator of the United States, Victoria Rodessa!" Johnnie held his arms out in an exaggerated gesture, welcoming her to the stage as everyone in the crowd jumped to their feet and the room erupted in cheers. A series of red, white, and blue balloons were unleashed from the ceiling as Victoria walked out into absolute pandemonium, waving one hand in the air and touching her heart with the other to signal her gratitude. She turned her head just enough to ensure Johnnie saw the roll of her eyes. She hated the balloons, thought they were corny, and had said so many, many times. Johnnie responded with a wink and walked offstage.

Over a year and a half ago, Victoria's team had completed its exploration into the viability of her run as a candidate for the US Senate. With the average age of those in the Senate being sixty-three, at forty-four, Victoria would be one of the youngest to hold the office. The polling had been good—great, in fact. So, after signing on to the idea and after much discussion with family and close friends, the next and immediate step for Victoria had been to hire a campaign manager. Her team had insisted on Johnnie. For the amount of money the campaign was paying him, Victoria had decided to loosen the reins and defer to him on most campaign matters. Her team had been right, though. Johnnie was good. She was up in the polls.

"Thank you, everyone. Thank you." Waving and smiling, Victoria waited for the cheering and clapping to die down. "Thank you for taking time out of your busy schedules to come out tonight to support my run for the United States Senate. We're heading into the final three days of our campaign, and we are ahead in the polls!" More cheers and clapping. "We have been endorsed by the top newspapers in the state and by the governor. And, just a few minutes ago, I received a call from the president of the United States, wishing our campaign well on Tuesday!" The crowd went wild at that one, as she knew they would. The current president was one of the most beloved heads of state the country had elected over the last twenty years. "You all know how important it is to get everyone out to vote on Tuesday, and . . ."

"V . . . V . . . V . . ."

Victoria heard her nickname being chanted in a weird whisper-yell coming from stage left. Out of the corner of her eye, she saw Jenny, one of her best friends and law partner, feverishly waving at her and gesturing with a slice of her hand across her neck in a straight line—the universal sign for *cut*.

Jesus. I'm not even a quarter of the way into my speech.

As Victoria tried to juggle maintaining audience connection with a level of consciousness about what was occurring offstage, Paulina, the campaign's PR and communications director, walked onto the stage from the wings, smiling, though there was a slight look of bewilderment in her big brown eyes.

"Okay, everyone," Paulina said as she grabbed the lapel mike off Victoria and moved it to her dress. "Victoria has a full schedule of interviews to do this evening." Paulina flashed her incredible smile. "She'll be around for your questions later this evening, and so will her staff. In the meantime, enjoy the food and drink and get ready to name our girl as the next senator from the great state of Illinois." She raised Victoria's hand in a typical fighter's victory salute and nodded to Jenny.

Victoria was pissed as she walked offstage. She'd had so much to say tonight. All of it substantive. She had wanted to emphasize the key parts of her plan for Illinois before the final few days of voting. "Jenny, what the hell is going on?"

"Just walk. Smile. Don't talk," Jenny ordered as she steered her by the elbow into a small anteroom off the stage and shut the door.

"Jenny, what the hell?"

Jenny held up her phone so Victoria could read the screen. Victoria grabbed the phone and scrolled through a series of breaking news stories before looking at Jenny. "Oh my God! When did this happen?"

"Five minutes after you took the stage. No question it was timed."

"This is not true," Victoria stated, looking at Jenny for her reaction and any sign that her friend might have doubts.

"Of course it's not true. But, while I've only had a chance to glance at the allegations, they appear detailed and specific. Unless we get to the bottom of it quickly and respond, it will impact the campaign. My best estimate is we've got no more than forty-eight hours to clean this up. That takes us to Sunday evening, which is dangerously close to the final day of voting on Tuesday. I've called the team. They're waiting at the hotel." Jenny threw Victoria's coat around her shoulders and began to steer her toward the back exit.

"I'd rather we head to my home," Victoria said. "It's secure and gated."

"Not a chance, V. The insanity will increase tenfold there."

"What insanity?" Victoria let the *ee* trail off as the back-stage door was flung open to the frigid Chicago evening and reporters crammed the opening like a swarm of locusts.

"Did you do it?"

"What's your defense?"

"Are you stopping your campaign?"

The reporters launched their random questions through the doorway, while cameras flashed in Victoria's eyes.

"This insanity," Jenny said under her breath. "Let's go. Do not stop. Do not answer questions."

Victoria kept her head down and flipped up the faux-fur collar of her coat. She could feel Jenny on her ass as they hunched behind a security guard who was bullying his way through the throng to the open door of the waiting limousine.

As the car pulled away, Victoria laid her hand on Jenny's arm, about to speak. She was met with a slight shake of her head and a nod at the driver. Victoria understood. It was the longest ten-minute ride of her life.

CHAPTER
2

A S SOON AS Victoria and Jenny walked into the campaign suite at the hotel, their normally sophisticated and calm team vocally climbed over one another to get the answers they each needed to do their jobs. Paulina's Southern accent was the first to cut through the cacophony. "I need our story and fast. The press is eating us alive. It's already breaking news on all the cable channels."

Originally from New Orleans, Paulina had been Victoria's first official hire after Johnnie and was invaluable to her campaign. She was adept at using her intelligence, determination, and Southern charm to disarm even the most ardent of Victoria's critics. With a white mother and a Black father, she spoke with conviction on racial issues and had a knack for saying the right thing at the right time. She had been key to the current president's victory and, for the first two years of his presidency, had assumed the role of communications director. Knowing she had at least two more years to bask in the glow of a grateful president, Paulina resigned her West Wing post and opened a public relations and communications firm. Nothing quite guaranteed success like a recommendation from the White House.

"I expect the story to be viral within the hour," Tulane spoke up. "Social media is already having a field day. The trending hashtag is #jurytampering. I need to counter with our story." Tulane ran social media and branding for Victoria. He and Paulina had met while working on the presidential campaign and had become fast friends. His six-foot frame, shock of white hair, and dark-chocolate skin made him stand out in any crowd. It had been a coup to get both Paulina and Tulane on her team. Granted, he and Paulina cost an arm and a leg, but they were worth every penny.

The final member of the team was Robert. A straitlaced, never-without-a-tie, balding, white lawyer in his late fifties, Robert specialized in employment, election law and fundraising. He had a quick wit and a very, very dry sense of humor. "We've got to be extremely careful with everything we say to the press or on social media. We're in a delicate dance with these accusations coming from this judge. He's a solid no-nonsense jurist who is as clean as a whistle. The campaign is fucked if he continues with this line of attack."

The room quieted, and everyone looked at Jenny after Robert's remark. While it was what they all were thinking, no one but Robert would have said it out loud. As the liaison between the team and Victoria, Jenny understood from years of trial work that once panic overtook a group, it was hard to quell. She also knew her outward demeanor would color the reaction of her audience. If the team captain panicked, everyone would follow suit. In the world of politics, people like Paulina and Tulane easily jumped ship to avoid the career killer of being associated with a failed campaign. She knew the next few minutes were crucial.

"Everyone, take a seat, please," Jenny said in her calmest and most authoritative trial voice. "Go ahead, V," she said, nodding to Victoria while she took a seat herself to allow Victoria center stage.

"Thank you, Jenny." Victoria walked to the corner of the room so she could make eye contact with every member of her team. "After fifteen months of working closely with me, you all, each and every one of you, know me exceedingly well. You have also come to know my close circle of friends and family, one of whom is Jenny, of course." She looked at her good friend. "Whatever happens, you must know that I consider you"—she turned her head slowly to look at each person in the room—"part of my inner circle and my dear friends."

"Victoria, if you're about to admit something, I suggest you, Jenny, and I head to a separate room to preserve any privileges and so that I can get my head around the facts to determine whether the situation is as bad as you think," Robert said in his monotone and soul-crushing fashion.

"What? Robert, no," Jenny responded, unable to stop the roll of her eyes at his constant pessimism.

"You can relax, Robert," Victoria broke in before the always present tension between Robert and Jenny could escalate. "I'm not going to confess, because there is nothing to admit. Everything in that story is false." A palpable sigh of relief circulated around the room, and the strained looks visibly softened.

"While none of us doubt you, I'm sorry, but we need more to go on than just your word," Paulina interrupted.

"She's right," Tulane added. "Social media feeds on bad news. To counter, we'll need more than your denial, which, of course, we'll get out right away. We'll need to figure out who did this and expose them to the world."

"That son of a bitch," Robert said, looking at his phone. "Take the television off mute." Paulina grabbed the remote from the coffee table and aimed it at the TV.

They all listened as Steven Dunne III, Victoria's opponent, put on a show for the media. "She needs to turn herself in and report to the authorities immediately. This is serious.

As an officer of the court, she has an obligation to uphold the highest standards of the legal profession, and as a candidate for the US Senate, she owes it to her supporters. As we speak, my team is reporting her to the legal bars of every state where she has a license. We are requesting immediate suspension of her ability to practice law and that she step down as managing partner of her firm."

"Asshole," Jenny directed at the television. "What about innocent until proven guilty?"

Paulina said, "Victoria, I've now got five requests from major networks to have you on air to answer these charges. What do you want to do?"

"Our response is 'no comment' right now," Robert interjected. "We need to figure out what evidence we do or don't have, and we cannot do interviews without it."

Paulina and Tulane shook their heads in unison. "If we do that, she may as well withdraw right now," Tulane said. "And if she takes that route, I'm sorry, but both Paulina and I would need to quit the campaign immediately. Our careers would never recover."

"Stop," Victoria interrupted, sounding calmer than she felt. "First, I will not answer these charges with 'no comment.' Second, we will go on air tonight and deny all charges. Paulina, for the next thirty minutes, I'll need you to pepper me with questions, refine my responses, and get me interview ready. Tulane, you'll be able to get enough out of our practice runs to post snippets on social media." She looked at each of them in turn as she gave out assignments. "Robert, stop this interference with my right to practice law. They need more than accusations to pull my licenses, and my opponent knows that. Please remind the bar committees of their due process obligations. Then get the name of this foreperson. While I have a vague memory of her, it was seventeen years and many trials ago. Find out where she lives and how and when she re-ported this bullshit to the judge. Oh, and I want to meet with her. Arrange it. She spoke with the judge, so I want the same courtesy. Jenny, stay with me."

As the meeting ended and the noise in the room began to build as each team member worked to tackle their assignments, Victoria pulled Jenny close and quietly said what they were both thinking. "If we don't get to the bottom of this, every-thing we've built will be ruined." Jenny only nodded, knowing her statement was true.

CHAPTER

3

THE LIGHTS IN the room were punishingly bright. Despite constant reassurances from Johnnie and Paulina that she looked fabulous on camera, Victoria vainly worried that some random and unsightly line on her neck or forehead would be highlighted and that would be all anyone would talk about afterward. "Thank God for Botox," she said as she squeezed Jenny's arm and smiled in an effort to relieve some of the tension.

"I personally love the fact that no one knows if I just don't care or if I'm happy or angry, since I have only minimal function in my forehead thanks to that product. Some call it overdone. I call it perfect," Jenny replied, running with Victoria's effort to restore some calm. They had handled over a dozen jury trials together, and there was little more character revealing than the strain of running large, complex, emotionally charged trials. They knew how the other ticked, and each had strengths the other needed. When united on a purpose, they were like a well-oiled machine.

Victoria lowered her voice to just above a whisper and stepped closer to Jenny to ensure no one could hear. "I need you to find a lawyer who specializes in white-collar crime and who is part of the Washington crowd. Someone who knows the ins and outs of the process of nominating federal judges and who was part of the scene when Judge Moran was nominated and approved by the Senate." She took a deep breath. "I want you to use all your connections and hire the best of the best. Find out who that is and get them on board yesterday."

"You're making me nervous, V. You've got both Robert and me on your team. Why would you want more lawyers?"

"Whoever is pulling this string knows what they're doing. They've got heavy hitters involved. We're up against—or rather, *I'm* up against—one of the most respected federal judges in the country. We need someone heavily connected in DC and to the federal judge nominating stream. Someone who has vetted judges and knows the process. Preferably someone who was involved in the vetting of this judge." She kept her gaze steady on Jenny's. "Use all your connections and call our DC and New York managing partners to get some names. Then vet them."

"Jenny, Victoria, it's time," Paulina called from across the room, where she stood chatting with the news anchor. They'd quickly created an interview set in the hotel suite so Victoria could avoid the swarm of the press. The news team had brought in tall, angled lights, two cameras, boom poles, and lavalier mics, complete with the necessary personnel to run the equipment. Cables large and small crisscrossed the room. Assistants and producers scurried around checking the accoutrements to ensure everything was in working order.

Nodding toward Paulina to acknowledge she'd heard, Victoria grabbed Jenny's arm, giving one more instruction. "Oh, and have Robert find out if we can use campaign funds to pay for this hotshot attorney or if I need to use my personal funds. The last thing I want is to start my term with a scandal about improper use of campaign funds."

"Got it. I'll start after you finish this interview."

"Here goes nothing and everything," Victoria said as she walked toward Paulina. Smoothing any sign of a wrinkle from her light-gray designer dress, she walked around the cameras and stepped over the tangle of wires toward two heavily cushioned chairs.

"It's a pleasure to meet you, Ms. Rodessa." Candace Sheridan Smith used the full wattage of her famous smile, but Victoria knew she was quickly sizing up the subject of her newest story. Along with her smile, Candace's intellect, wit, and unique ability to weave the news of the day into a story with historical ties were the assets that allowed her to earn a seven-figure salary. The ratings at the cable network had risen by 30 percent after Candace joined the team, and she continued to be the star host of *The Reveal with Candace*, the most watched cable news show. "I'm sorry to meet you under these circumstances. I was hoping to get your first interview after your election victory. But here we are," Candace said with a slight shrug.

Victoria had often watched Candace on the nightly news and had enjoyed her in-depth investigative stories. She was smart and clever. Paulina had done a great job summarizing her interrogation style and preparing Victoria. Paulina had also drilled into Victoria that her one goal was to prevent the audience from leaving the interview with any doubt about her innocence or with any sound bites or half-finished thoughts that could be misconstrued. As her communications director, Paulina had taught Victoria two rules: be forthright and do not give half answers. Half answers allowed the audience or the interviewer to fill in the blanks, and no one ever filled in those blanks with happy thoughts. *There is no Tinkerbell in PR*, Paulina often said, meaning that no one would think happy thoughts if you failed to answer a question or were nonresponsive.

"I'm happy to meet you as well, as I've admired and watched your career. I look forward to our chat, and I'm confident you'll get your chance to interview me during my term as senator."

"I appreciate your confidence, especially at this difficult time," Candace responded, probably hoping to win a bit of trust from Victoria. "Before we go live, are there any areas that are off-limits?" Candace held up her hand to stop Victoria from responding immediately. "However, that doesn't mean I'll agree to any limitations. It's simply an offer."

Victoria appreciated the cleverness of Candace's question. If the interviewee answered with a specific off-limit topic, it would give Candace a bull's-eye for the interview or follow-up questions. Fortunately, Paulina had prepared Victoria for this. Out of the corner of her eye, she saw Paulina slowly shaking her head back and forth.

Victoria cocked her head, looked Candace directly in the eyes, and smiled. "Nothing is off-limits, Candace. I have nothing to hide. Shall we begin?"

"Of course. Remember, we're live. No do-overs," Candace warned as she signaled to her production team that she was ready. "Good evening, this is Candace Sheridan Smith with breaking news on the fiercely contested race for the next senator from Illinois." As was her way, Candace launched into a brief history of the two candidates, their backgrounds, and even a snippet about the trial that was the subject of the allegations. "Now here with me to discuss the allegations is Victoria Rodessa, the Democratic candidate in one of the most hotly contested US Senate races in the country." Turning from a direct camera shot, she looked at Victoria. "Welcome, Ms. Rodessa, and thank you for taking the time to talk with me this evening, especially with all that is going on in your campaign."

"Of course. And please, call me Victoria."

Candace nodded and turned back to the camera. "For the folks at home who may not be aware of the latest breaking news, ninety minutes ago, Judge Moran, the chief judge of the Federal Court for the Northern District of Illinois, issued the following statement: 'As a federal judge and an officer of the court, I cannot stay silent. About seventeen years ago, Ms. Rodessa tried a case before a jury in my courtroom. She won over one hundred twenty million dollars for her clients. Two days ago, I was approached by the foreperson of the jury in that case. This person confessed that she had pushed the jury to rule in favor of Ms. Rodessa's clients because of illegal conduct by Ms. Rodessa. More will come out in the hours ahead. But for now, as the election is only days away, I wanted the voting public to know.'

"Ms. Rodessa—sorry, Victoria," Candace corrected as she saw Victoria was about to remind her, "Judge Moran is, as you well know, a respected jurist with a sterling reputation. He has lodged serious charges against you. Can you explain why the judge would make these allegations if they weren't true?"

"Judge Moran and I are very well acquainted, as I've made public during my campaign. I interned for the chief judge during my last two years of law school. In fact, he was one of several people who wrote letters of recommendation to Acker, Smith and McGowen, the law firm that hired me as an associate when I graduated from law school."

"Yes, and you're now the managing partner of that firm and own significant equity in it. One could argue that the shared history between you and the judge makes his allegations even more convincing."

Victoria looked at Paulina and Jenny, who were standing behind the camera she was facing. They stood there on purpose to be able to communicate with her, albeit with eye contact and gestures only, should they want to try to convey a message. Both were nodding their heads, signaling it was time.

After taking a deep breath to steady herself, Victoria said, "I can't tell you what the judge's motives are or why he would come up with such a blatant lie." Victoria almost choked using that accusatory word in the same sentence as the name of one of the most powerful sitting judges in the country. "Nothing in his statement is true. I have never even spoken to a member of a jury while a trial is ongoing, let alone *tampered* with a jury."

Candace sat back and looked directly into the camera, widening her eyes just a bit to emphasize to her audience what a coup of an interview she was conducting. The forerunner for the US Senate had just called the chief judge a liar. "Surely you aren't accusing the chief judge of lying. Perhaps it's a mis-understanding?" Candace asked, knowing full well Victoria had meant what she said but using repetition to whip up her audience.

"He is lying," Victoria answered firmly, looking into the camera. "To all my supporters, I want you to know that I will get to the bottom of this effort to derail my campaign and destroy my reputation. I intend to expose the perpetrators of this lie, win this Senate seat, and go on to represent the people of the great state of Illinois in Congress."

Candace looked almost giddy. After all, this promised to be easy headlines and ratings for her show for however long it took someone to figure out what was going on. "I appreciate you taking time out from what will undoubtedly be a very busy time for you and your team. Please come back and give us an update when you're ready."

"Thanks for having me. Oh, and one more thing." The cameras moved in on Victoria's face and dark-brown eyes. "Your Honor, and whoever else is behind this, I'm coming for you."

CHAPTER

4

"**S**HIT, VICTORIA," JENNY said as she and Paulina pulled Victoria into the back bedroom of the suite while the TV crew started to break down their equipment. "You were amazing. But that last little bit was not part of our run-through. Did you really need to threaten a federal judge?"

"Thanks. And I did not threaten him—I made a promise. You know very well my statement provides nowhere near the necessary elements to satisfy the federal statute for threatening government officials. It was clear from the context that it was about finding the truth." She shrugged. "Anyway, that's the least of my worries. If we can't get to the bottom of this, I'll be charged with jury tampering and lose my licenses to practice law, my shares and position in the firm, and my run for the Senate."

"You did great," Paulina said. "Tulane has already pushed out sound bites from the interview, and you're trending with positive support. Hashtag fightback is trending!

The door to the bedroom opened and closed softly. Without turning, Victoria knew who had entered from the smell of his cologne.

"Well, I see you're consistent. Still running into one mess after another. Can't you do a simple thing like run for Congress without falling into a shithole?" Armond asked as he shrugged off his coat, wet from the cold rain that had begun to fall. "And, while I know it's off topic and likely the wrong time to bring it up, when are you moving the headquarters of that ginormous firm you run to the West Coast? I see no need to keep it here in this frigid city anymore."

The tense atmosphere in the room lightened immediately. "Armond, what are you doing here? And how in the world did you get here?" Jenny asked, smiling as she watched Victoria and Armond embrace.

"Diverted my plane to this godforsaken city of ice and snow when I saw the headlines," Armond answered, smiling at Jenny. He ran a hand over Victoria's hair, then held her at arm's length so he could see her face. "And how are you, my pet?"

"Oh, you know. Same old, same old. Fighting with federal judges, trying to keep a campaign afloat, and fending off criminal charges. Anything new on your end?"

Just then, the door flew open and snapped back against the wall, making everyone jump. "I hate to break this up, but we've got to move quickly," Robert nearly shouted. "I've located the foreperson. We're trying to get in touch with her, but she's not answering her phone. We know where she lives. I suggest we go visit her now and see if she'll answer the door if she knows it's you."

"What's her name, Robert? I vaguely remember what she looks like but not her name," Victoria said, resting her head against Armond's chest, remembering how comforting it was and missing the force they had been.

"Spanberger. Mary Ellen Spanberger," Robert answered. "Does that ring a bell? Do you recall speaking with her?

Any little thing might be helpful before we talk with her. Apparently, she works as ground crew at the airport."

"I recall she took copious notes, at least that's what I thought from the amount of writing she did. She listened intently. That's it," Victoria said. "Oh, and I do remember being surprised that she was the foreperson."

Jenny chimed in, "Why were you surprised?"

"She seemed a bit isolated from the other jurors during the trial. You know the type. Other jurors speak to one another while waiting for the judge or on the way in or out for breaks. She always seemed to stay above the fray."

"Well, she's not above the fray now." Jenny grabbed her laptop from the desk. "I'm coming with you."

"Actually, Jenny, I think it best that you work on retaining that Washington lawyer. I don't want to spook her with an army of folks showing up at her door late at night."

Noticing that Armond had picked up his wet coat, Victoria touched his arm. "Armond, I know we have a lot to catch up on, and I can't thank you enough for coming, but would you mind digging into your connections to work with Jenny on a project I gave her?"

Looking disappointed but understanding it was not the time to get into their personal business, Armond set his coat back onto the chair. Always with a glass-half-full outlook, he smiled at Victoria. "That's why I came. Anything and any connections I have are at your disposal." Turning to Jenny, he said, "Jenny, fill me in and let's get this nonsense under control."

"Thanks," Victoria said, smiling up at him. "Jenny, if you don't mind, introduce Armond to the rest of the team and make sure they know what he means to the firm and to me personally."

"Got it. Now go, before someone else gets to this woman first."

As Victoria was heading out the door with Robert and their security team, she heard Armond say, "Oh no, no, no. We are not drinking this swill. Can one of you connect me with the suite concierge?"

Smiling, Victoria shut the door and followed Robert and their security team to the waiting car.

CHAPTER

5

MARY ELLEN SAT in her recliner, comfy-cozy in her favorite furry socks and warmest sweats. The frigid rain had just begun to turn to heavy, wet snow, and she snuggled under her softest blanket, ready to watch one of her favorite television shows. Just as she was dozing off, she received a series of group texts from her sons.

Mom, what is going on?

Why didn't you tell us about this?

She had no idea what they were talking about, but long ago, she'd told them she refused to engage in what they referred to as conversation via text. She did not respond, turned out the lights, and fell asleep with the TV on.

CHAPTER

6

CAL DURHAM WAS slightly buzzed but still functional, having just returned home from a reception at the White House. He was working with the new administration to find suitable prospects for federal judgeships that were open or opening soon. This administration intended to hire the most federal judges in recent history and had launched its effort with a bang. His plate looked to be full for the next two years at least.

Phones had not been allowed in the highly secure West Wing gathering, which he preferred. It meant that, just like the old days, the invited guests and administration officials could actually enjoy the moment and focus on one another. It also meant that, at least for a few hours, he didn't need to watch some idiot posing at a ridiculous angle to take a selfie with a cabinet member or congressperson.

"Narcissists," he said out loud to no one, chuckling, appreciating the irony of sending his social media team a few of the shots he'd taken of himself heading into the West Wing. *If you can't beat 'em . . .* Cal knew better than to buck a trend that got him noticed and got him more clients than he could shake a stick at. Never in his wildest dreams did he think that a farm boy from Nebraska would make it to Washington, let alone own a Virginia penthouse and a summer house in the Berkshires and have direct access to the president. But here he was, and he was loving life.

When he finally checked his phone, there was one text.

Urgent potential client matter. Call to discuss. Do not wait until the morning!

Looking at his Patek Philippe watch, given to him by a grateful client who was now a federal judge, he saw it was past eleven.

He pushed the speed dial on his phone and soon heard Claire Anderson's always cheery voice on the other end. "I thought that would pique your interest. How was it, and when do I get to tag along to one of these shindigs?"

"How about when you gain enough sense to stop texting me at ungodly hours?" Cal snarled.

"Believe me, you're going to be happy I did," Claire responded, unfazed by Cal's gruff demeanor. She loved working for him. She had wanted to work at the Capitol ever since she was a little girl. Lucky for Claire, whenever Cal needed a new associate, he prioritized candidates from Nebraska, as he knew it wasn't one of the states the Washington elite pulled from. And although he would never admit it, he had a soft spot for helping others. Cal liked to tell Claire he had pulled her from obscurity. *Well, not total obscurity,* she thought. She had, after all, been top of her graduating class at Harvard Law, having earned a full scholarship that gave her a one-way ticket out of the Nebraska cornfields. *The Cornhusker state. Sheesh.* She shook her head to get back on track.

"Are you still with me, or have you traveled into one of your private fairy tales?" Cal asked, used to her mind drifting to some fantasy or another during the oddest of times. "Come on, damn it. It's working toward midnight, and God knows if you'll turn into a pumpkin and I'll never hear whatever it is you have to say."

"Okay, okay." Claire laughed. "You got me. Have you been paying attention to the Senate race out of Illinois? It's hotly contested. The newcomer against the entrenched." Claire didn't wait for his response. "Anyway, the shit hit the fan tonight, and they want to hire you. They want you in Chicago first thing."

Cal rubbed his eyes and took a deep breath, using every bit of patience he could find to not hang up. "Who, Claire? Who wants to hire me? And what shit hit the fan?"

Claire scrunched her nose, a physical reaction to the bit of dread she was feeling about explaining to her boss all she had already done without his go-ahead. "I checked conflicts. We're clear. We can take this on, so I said yes and booked us on the eight a.m. flight," she said quickly, rushing to get it all out. "Our client is Victoria Rodessa. Judge Moran published a statement at about nine thirty p.m. our time accusing Ms. Rodessa of jury tampering and throwing a trial." Claire stopped and waited for the explosion.

"I'm reading the news feed now. Hold on," Cal responded, shocking Claire by not lambasting her for taking on a client without discussing it with him first. "Holy shit! I knew that name sounded familiar. I vetted this judge for his position more than twenty years ago. He was clean. But that doesn't place me in a position of conflict," Cal said, talking more to himself than to Claire. "Okay, anything else?"

"She gave an interview tonight to Candace Sheridan Smith. It's being run ad nauseam on all the news channels. You should watch it before we meet her in the morning."

"Will do. See you at the airport. Oh, and for a farm girl from Nebraska, good work." He smiled as he hung up the phone.

CHAPTER

7

THE HOUSE WAS a typical Chicago bungalow, located near Midway Airport. Orangish brick, concrete stairs with a black iron railing leading to the front door, a cookie-cutter but well-manicured yard, and bars over the windows. The houses on the block were all made from the same mold. Many of the homes were still dressed for the Halloween that had just passed. In the yards were orange lights, skeletons, gravestones, and Victoria's pet peeve, blow-up "scary" figures.

"Not much imagination from this developer," Robert said, looking out his window as their car pulled up to the dark house.

Victoria snorted. "I grew up in this exact type of neighborhood and loved every minute of it. Close-knit neighbors, all of whom work hard and are proud of what they do. Every year, we had a Fourth of July parade. We'd decorate our bikes, put some paint on our faces, and ride behind some neighbor's car while the other parents stood on the sidewalk, cheering and clapping. We thought we were amazing."

Victoria checked the time as she sat looking at the house. Robert, her security detail, and the driver waited for her direction. "Robert, I think we should come back in the morning.

She's obviously either sleeping or isn't at home. If she's sleeping, I don't want to scare her by pounding on her door at this hour."

"I don't disagree with you, but every minute we wait, your campaign gets a little closer to being flushed down the toilet. We really don't have a choice. And this might be the only chance to speak with her before the press and the investigators get to her."

Victoria sighed. "Good point. Okay, let's go." Leaning forward and speaking across the spacious limousine, she asked, "James, would you come with us just in case?"

James, a man of few words who ran the campaign's security, nodded. "You weren't getting out of the car without me, ma'am."

The group of three stepped out into the quiet street, silent but for the electric hum of the streetlights that shone from each corner and cast a creepy light over the yards. *Maybe it's the decorations that make it feel so unnerving*, Victoria thought. It had been an unseasonably hot summer with little rain, and bits and pieces of the brown, fried grass on the front lawns showed through under the light coating of snow that had just begun to fall. The frozen grass crunched under their feet as they crossed the lawn toward the house.

"I think we should come back in the morning. She's clearly sleeping." Victoria thought twice about her decision as she nodded at the large front window showing nothing but black on the other side. "I wouldn't be happy if a group of strangers banged on my door in the middle of the night. In fact, I would call the police."

"We can't afford to wait." Robert opened the glass-topped screen door and lightly tapped on the wooden door. Silence. "If I found her with just a bit of help from my cop contacts, the press won't be far behind." Knocking a bit louder, he stood on his tiptoes to peek through the rectangular glass window built into the wooden door. "No one's moving."

"Of course not. She's sleeping," Victoria said. "I'm making an executive decision. Everyone back in the car. We'll come back first thing in the morning. That's only about six hours away."

"First thing in the morning needs to be no later than five a.m.," Robert muttered.

"Okay then, five hours away." Victoria took one last look through the picture window before she turned to walk to the limousine. "Now let's go."

CHAPTER

8

IT WAS PITCH-BLACK outside when Victoria woke at 3:30 a.m., having gotten only a few hours of sleep. After taking a quick shower, she had just finished twisting her thick hair into a French knot at the nape of her neck when she heard a light knock on her door. Peeking through the peephole while unlocking the bolt and chain, she saw Jenny, as expected. "Thank God you brought coffee. Oh, and a pastry too. You are my savior." Victoria inhaled deeply as she smelled the coffee and glanced in the bag. Then she looked at Jenny more closely. "Wait, did you even sleep? Isn't that what you were wearing last night?"

"I did not sleep, nor have I showered, which I will be doing as soon as I bring you up to speed. And yes, I know you appreciate it, and you can pay me back with a weekend trip to some fabulous spa after you win your seat in the Senate."

"Done. Now tell me."

"First, the woman doesn't even have a speeding ticket. Her mortgage is paid, she does not gamble, and she isn't part of a swingers' group. There are no lawsuits by or against her. No taxes owed. Nothing. She's a single mom who, it appears, has worked her ass off raising her boys on her own. She's worked for the past twenty-five years as ground crew at the airport."

"What about her ex? Is he still around?"

"The story is that he died years ago. The boys never met their father, and we could not find anyone who has ever heard her talk about him," Jenny said. "There are no documents that mention him, at least none that we've found at this point. We found no record of her ever having been married."

"So we have no motive and no dirt. Just a hardworking, South Side, single mom doing her best on her own. Just great. That will play well with the press and the voters when I call her a liar." Victoria made some frustrated doodles in her notebook, as there was nothing of substance to jot down.

"We do have some good news. Cal Durham has been retained and will be landing in a few hours. He's asked for a meeting as soon as he arrives at the hotel."

"He's the connected DC lawyer?"

"He is. Not only has he worked in the political arena for years, but he's been heavily involved in choosing lawyers to recommend to the White House to fill federal judgeships. He's worked for both Republican and Democratic presidents and is highly respected. If there's dirt on an attorney or a judge, he'll know it or at least know where to look for it," Jenny said. "Oh, fun fact. He is the one who vetted Judge Moran for the federal bench and helped shepherd him through the Senate confirmation process."

"Jenny, do you think that presents a conflict of some sort?" Victoria asked. "I mean, he obviously knows all there is to know about Moran and found him to be such an upstanding attorney that he recommended him for the federal bench."

"No, I don't. And if there was a conflict, he would have declined the representation."

Hearing a knock on the door, Jenny cocked her head.

"That'll be Robert," Victoria said, answering Jenny's unspoken question. "We're headed back to her home in about"—she looked at her watch—"an hour. We didn't speak with her because it was after midnight and she was not answering her door. Robert, of course, wanted to pound the shit out of it until she answered," Victoria explained as she went to open her door.

Instead, she found Armond, Paulina, and Tulane standing in the doorway. "What are you doing here? Where's Robert?"

Armond pushed everyone into Victoria's room and shut the door. "There's no easy way to say this." He took a deep breath. "Spanberger was found dead about two hours ago. After she didn't answer her sons' texts and calls, they asked one of her neighbors to check on her. They found the door unlocked and her body on the floor."

"You've got to be kidding me. This is unbelievable." Victoria's mind was racing as the import of the news kicked in. Then she put a hand over her mouth and murmured, "Poor woman."

"I'm not kidding. And guess whose fingerprints the police found all over her front door?"

"Oh my God. Robert."

Nodding, Armond continued, "The police are with him now. I've called in a favor, and one of the best criminal defense lawyers in the state is with him as well."

"I was with Robert. I'm sure I touched her door."

"You did. They have your prints as well," Armond said. "They're working on Robert first. If I had to guess, it's to get him to turn on the big fish—you."

"I have nothing to hide. We did nothing wrong. I'm happy to speak with the police."

Armond placed his hands on Victoria's shoulders. "I have no doubt. But they are looking for an answer to a suspicious death. Do not speak with them until you've spoken with your new lawyer, who is landing in a few hours."

Jenny turned to Paulina and Tulane. "I need you two to develop a statement to issue to the press. Can you knock it out in the next fifteen minutes? Innocent, of course. Happy to co-operate, et cetera. Let me know when it's ready for my review."

"We can do that," Tulane said. "But it still leaves unanswered the question everyone will be asking: Why were Victoria's prints found on her door?"

Looking up at Armond, Victoria thought for a moment. Then she snapped her fingers. "Give them the answer. Tell them I was after the truth. I never tampered with a jury, and I wanted to find out why she said I did. When we got there, there was no answer. Neither my nor Robert's prints will be found in the house or on the body. Plus, James was with us. He can vouch for us, and, if he's willing, let the press talk to him."

"Victoria, I think you should run this by Cal Durham first. He may have another idea," Jenny suggested.

"Let's run with this statement," Armond interjected. "Things are happening by the second, and she can't be silent on this for hours while waiting for this lawyer to develop a strategy. It would look bad."

"I agree," Paulina chimed in. "Any void will be filled with negative." She ushered Tulane toward the door to the rest of the suite. "We'll draft the statement. Keep us in the loop so we're not blindsided by anything."

CAL HAD KEPT countless notes over the years on the prospective judges he had interviewed. He had been meticulous in his scrutiny of any prospect he presented to the White House. The last thing Cal wanted was for some unfortunate detail to pop up mid-Senate confirmation hearing that he hadn't uncovered. His notes were his backup. Since the judges received lifetime appointments, Cal was smart enough to know that somewhere along the way, one or two of them would get into trouble, and he wanted proof that he'd either found it and warned the committee or that the issue had developed after the judge's appointment.

Cal finished pouring through his notes on Moran just as the plane touched down in Chicago. "Nothing in here concerns me about the judge." Cal turned to Claire. "Anything on Rodessa?"

"You've heard of her, right?" Claire asked incredulously.

Cal raised one eyebrow. "I have not heard of her, no. And if I had, I would not have bothered to ask. Now, are you going to fill me in or continue with the theatrics your generation is so pleased to unleash on anyone who has not seen the newest trending cat video?"

"Well, they are funny." Claire smiled and looked over, expecting him to enjoy her humor, but instead she saw utter annoyance. "Fill you in sounds like the best option," she muttered, opening her laptop. "Okay. Rodessa has been in the thick of things and comes out ahead each time. She was raised by a single mother on the South Side of Chicago, attended one of the best law schools on an academic scholarship, graduated second in her class, and was snapped up by the powerhouse firm Acker, Smith and McGowen. While there's a lot to her story, in a nutshell, after a few hurdles at the firm, she began her own successful practice and later ended up the majority owner and managing partner of Acker. Amazing, really. Like a female John Wayne, or whoever it is your generation and gender admire."

Seeing Cal's eyebrow rise again, Claire refocused. "Her Senate run had her six points ahead of her opponent until yesterday, when this story dropped. She's sinking fast in the polls and has little time to recover. Our job, as instructed by her close friend and personal attorney, Jenny Acker, is to, and I quote, 'get to the bottom of this shithole, clear her name, and save her run for the Senate.'"

"What about the judge?"

"I tried to connect with him before we left DC. I used his personal cell number you gave me and left a voicemail saying that you would like to speak with him first thing this morning. I said that we're representing Ms. Rodessa. No response yet. I doubt he'll call."

Just then, Claire's phone rang. Holding up a finger to warn Cal she was taking the call, she answered. "This is Claire." After a few moments, she said, "Got it. Yes, we can handle that aspect as well. We'll be there as soon as traffic allows."

"What's going on?"

"The foreperson who accused Victoria was found dead in her home early this morning. Victoria's and her campaign lawyer's fingerprints are all over the deceased's front door. Both of them were there late last night because they wanted to speak with her about the accusations before anyone else got to her. She didn't answer, the house was dark, and they didn't want to wake her, so they left."

Cal smiled.

"What in the world are you smiling about? This case went from potential slander involving a federal judge and a Senate candidate and jury tampering to murder in less than eight hours."

"Indeed," was the only response Claire received.

CHAPTER 10

"HOW'S OUR BOY holding up?" the man asked, standing to his full six foot six inches. As chair of a conglomerate holding company consisting of hotels, cruise lines, shipping, and oil, he was used to commanding a room.

"Your instincts were right. He was a bit of a mess, and the news about the woman's murder didn't help," one of the men assigned to special projects responded. "We sent him a note reminding him, in no uncertain terms, what would happen if he deviated from the plan. Our bet is he'll hold for the next twenty-four hours, enough to give your man a solid lead in the election. At that point, this should all move off the front page, and we'll be able to deal with him as well."

"Keep me posted."

CHAPTER

11

T IME WAS TICKING, and Cal was anxious to get to the hotel to meet his new client. After a solid sixty minutes of slow-moving traffic, they finally turned onto Michigan Avenue only to be faced with a complete standstill. Horns were blaring, no one was moving, and the hotel was six blocks away.

"That's it. Get out," Cal said to Claire, leaning forward to tell the driver to pull over. Claire had expected as much and was happy to walk after sitting on the plane. As they pulled their luggage from the trunk, Claire looked at her phone. "They're wondering what our ETA is," Claire said after reading the text.

"Tell them five minutes. Let's move."

Entering the lobby, they followed the directions they had been provided and took the private elevator up to the campaign suites. As soon as the elevator doors opened, they were immediately drawn into what appeared to be organized chaos, with people crisscrossing one another while on phones or laptops and juggling coffee or breakfast.

Jenny was the first to see them. "Cal and Claire, welcome. Let me introduce you to Victoria." Then she continued the introductions with everyone else on the team. Looking at the group assembled in the suite, she suggested, "If I can ask you all to step out and return in an hour? Why don't you grab some breakfast, take it next door to the adjoining suite, and we'll fill you in when we finish."

As the rest of the campaign staff picked up their phones, laptops, and bags to leave, Paulina turned to Victoria. "What do you want to do about further statements to the press?"

"Hold them for now," Cal interjected. "We'll give you something to get out within the next few hours. I'd like it to be a bit more substantive than just a blanket statement about innocence."

Paulina looked to Victoria, who nodded in agreement.

As the last of the team left the room, except for Jenny and Armond, Victoria turned to Cal. "Nice to meet you. I've heard great things about you, but frankly the most intriguing and important from my perspective is that you vetted and suggested Moran for his federal judgeship. We have precious little time to get this figured out. What have you got for us about the judge?"

"Nice to meet you as well. I've heard you've gotten in and out of a few scrapes along the way. Seems that trouble follows you."

Victoria felt her blood begin to boil, but she had no time to deal with an ignorant statement. Whatever his issues were, all she wanted from him was his information. "Again, Mr. Durham, what have you got for us about the judge?"

"Nothing on the judge. He was clean when I nominated him and has remained clean, as far as I know."

"Well, let me enlighten you," Victoria said, picking up her phone to leave while giving Jenny a dirty look, clearly conveying her displeasure with her pick of a lawyer. "I have never tampered with a jury, threatened a juror, or even looked at a juror outside of the courtroom during a trial. It's a ridiculous accusation. So someone's lying, and it's not me. Telling me that the judge has remained clean is a problem. Perhaps you're not the right fit."

"A respected federal judge said he was told by a now dead foreperson that you communicated with her to improperly rig the outcome of a major trial. That's what the public is hearing. Getting angry because I have no dirt on the judge will help neither you nor your campaign. What we need to do," Cal said, pointing to Claire and himself, "is get to the judge and pull on whatever loose thread exists to figure out what happened, who is lying, and why."

"That leaves three people in the immediate equation," Victoria said. "Me, the judge, and the deceased. So the possibilities are that one or two of us are—or were—lying. I can assure you I am not lying. That leaves the judge or the deceased, or both."

"There could be others involved," Claire piped in, trying to reduce the tension. "I mean, you are running for Senate, and the story was released during one of your campaign rallies close to the eve of the election. It's unlikely that was a coincidence. What about your opponent?"

"Oh, I agree there's a good chance my opponent is somehow involved. He's a billionaire and used to getting his own way. But the fastest way to prove that will be through those doing his dirty work. One of whom was murdered a few hours ago. So that leaves the judge. Now, Mr. Durham, either you and Claire believe me, or we go our separate ways." Victoria looked at her watch. "You have exactly two minutes to give me your answer."

Upon looking up, Victoria was annoyed to see Cal fiddling with a sugar packet to dump into his coffee. "Well, what's it going to be?" Victoria demanded.

"I have a few more questions before I give you my answer. May I continue?"

"Please do," Jenny said, placing her hand gently on Victoria's back, signaling for her friend to calm down and pull back. Jenny knew Victoria had a hot temper that was hard to shut down once ignited. But they had no time to find another lawyer of Cal's caliber.

"Look," Cal began, "we did not start off on the right foot. I apologize. But I need to push you a bit, as I'm sure you can understand as a trial lawyer."

"I do understand. However, we are not dealing with a typical case intake timeline where you can get your feet wet, sit back, think about your opinion, and come back for more," Victoria asserted. "We are under an incredible time crunch. If we don't get to the bottom of this in the next twenty-four to thirty-six hours, I will have to pull the plug on my campaign."

Cal nodded. "I understand."

Claire stepped in, knowing it was time to take some of the heat off her boss. "Because we're under a time crunch, I hope you don't mind if I get right to the point?"

"I do not. Please do."

"The trial. I know you won one hundred twenty million dollars for your clients. But what was it about, and how were you paid?" Claire took out her laptop, ready to take notes.

"It was a class action personal injury case. Years of pollutants had entered the groundwater from a manufacturing facility's seepage pit. The people who used that water downstream from the facility ended up with different cancers, the women experienced countless miscarriages or stillbirths, and their property values plummeted." Victoria shook her head, remembering the suffering her clients had endured. "I represented the plaintiffs and proved that the company executives knew that by dumping their waste into this pit, it was seeping into the groundwater and that they chose to do nothing about it for over twenty years. The jury agreed and awarded one of the largest compensatory and punitive damage verdicts at the time."

"Were you paid hourly or contingent?" Claire asked.

"We take those cases on a contingent fee basis."

Claire looked up from her laptop. "So—and forgive me for being blunt—an argument could be made that you had a real monetary motive to win this case and win it big versus the typical hourly fee case. Would you agree?"

"I would. But I never spoke to the foreperson or to any juror. My record is unblemished."

"Look, we believe you," Cal interjected. "The problem we have is that the judge's record is equally pristine."

Armond stepped forward. "Cal and Claire, I can certainly vouch for Victoria's character and work ethic. We have a long history together, as I was the partner she reported to when she was hired at Acker as a young associate. Since then, I've watched her scrupulously build that firm over the years. She's personally handled Renoir Productions' corporate work, my family's production company, for more than fifteen years. She is being framed."

"I appreciate your input, Mr. Renoir," Cal acknowledged.

"Armond, please."

"Armond. Now, we need to dig in. Jenny told us that your investigators have a report on the foreperson and that she appeared to be clean as well."

"I thought I would put them to use overnight. Here's their report." Armond handed the papers to Cal. "They have more to do, but I at least wanted to get whatever information was easily accessible on Ms. Spanberger. You are free to use my company's investigators; they are top-notch in ferreting stench out of a hole."

"I need to make a call," Cal announced as he pulled up his contact list in his phone and pressed the call button.

"You can have some privacy—" Jenny began, but Cal waved her off.

"No need; this is fine. Everyone can hear what I have to say."

They all waited in silence while Cal's ear was pressed to his phone. Jenny looked at Victoria and Armond and shrugged.

"Roger! Cal Durham here." Cal smiled, looking happy to hear the person on the other end of the call. "I'm fine, just fine. You?" Silence descended on the room again. Then Cal said, "I've seen you've made a bit of news. Before you respond, I must tell you that I am representing Ms. Rodessa in the matter you raised by your announcement last evening. I wanted you to hear it from me." Silence. "Yes, I am serious. And, of course, my first question to you is do you have counsel?" More silence. "Well then, I suggest you get an attorney, and I suggest that all parties search for the truth. My best to your family."

Hanging up, Cal looked around the room. "Well, Victoria, does that answer your question?"

"Not yet. Based on your knowledge of this judge, do you believe he would have made that announcement knowing it was false?"

"I knew the judge more than twenty years ago. People change. That's a fact." Cal shrugged. "But the man I knew would not have done this knowing it was false. However, one thing I've learned over the years is that there are no coincidences. This announcement was timed to ruin your Senate run. The unfortunate death of Ms. Spanberger is too coincidental when compared to the time you went to her home. Furthermore, you were an up-and-coming lawyer earning a significant salary at the time, so why would you have taken the chance of throwing a trial and tampering with a jury? None of it makes sense." Cal held out his hand toward Victoria.

"So I'm—I mean, *we're*—on your team," he said, nodding at Claire. "If you'll have us."

"Welcome aboard." Victoria smiled and grasped his hand. "Now, let's get to work."

CHAPTER

12

L ATE IN THE afternoon, Jerome and Anthony, the two Renoir Productions investigators, walked into the temporary office Armond had set up in an adjacent suite. "Armond, we've got the report on Spanberger's family."

"Great, go."

"The boys are sixteen years old and twins. They've been away at boarding school since they entered their freshman year. They never knew their father. From what we've gathered so far, their mother told them he died when they were babies, refused to give them any other information, and never spoke of him," Jerome reported. "According to the police investigation, the last time the boys spoke with their mother was Friday morning, prior to the judge's announcement. After her name leaked as the foreperson, they tried to reach her repeatedly, but she never returned their texts or calls."

Anthony continued, "We pulled all the background checks the airport and the FAA conducted over the years. There are a few red flags. See what you think." He tossed the report on the coffee table Armond was using as his desk.

Armond whistled as he read the report. "Wasn't this investigated further by the TSA or whatever federal agency conducts these investigations?"

"No. They stopped. We've since learned that they don't do a deep dive into personal financial wealth. They will investigate further only if there is significant debt or a criminal record," Anthony said, acknowledging Armond's expression. "We were surprised too. But apparently, if a potential employee or her family has money and no criminal background, then they are not worried about them being bribed to conduct some nefarious activity."

"Did her parents have money?"

"No. Her parents immigrated from the Czech Republic. They came to the United States separately when they were in their twenties, then met and married in Chicago. Her father used his skills as a woodworker and sold custom furniture out of a leased storefront. Her mother worked as a teacher for a short bit and then as ground crew at Midway," Jerome answered. "She's the one who got Mary Ellen her job. Although they supported themselves just fine, they were not wealthy. At this point, what you're reading in that report is not adding up."

"Come with me," Armond directed as he walked toward the suite next door, where Jenny, Cal, and Claire were gathered. Upon entering, he handed the report to Cal and introduced the two investigators. "Take a look at this report on the deceased. My guys will fill you in." He looked around the room. "Where's Victoria?"

Cal nodded to the far end of the room, where a bundle wrapped in a blanket was passed out on the sofa. "She hasn't really slept in almost twenty-four hours, so I insisted she lie down for a bit, and well . . ."

"I'm surprised she listened to you. But thanks." Armond walked over and stood looking down at her. He missed her terribly. It had been almost four years since they had gone in different directions after finally admitting to each other that they did not want the same things from life. Much to his surprise, he wanted marriage and children, and much to her surprise, she did not. Life had not been the same without Victoria, and he couldn't help but think that they had been too quick in their decision to part ways.

Victoria rolled over and yawned. "Hey, didn't anyone teach you at that fancy-pants prep school that it's rude to stare?"

Armond smirked. "As might be obvious to even the least astute observer, I ditched Interpersonal Skills 101."

"Shocking news." Victoria smiled, sitting up while pushing heavy locks of hair out of her face. "I'm famished." She checked her watch. "Everyone else must be too. I'll order a spread for everyone from room service. While I do that, would you mind gathering Cal and Claire and the troops for an update? I need to catch up."

"Happy to. My investigators found some interesting information about the deceased. I turned it over to Cal. But order the food, and we'll set up a meeting to begin in fifteen."

CHAPTER

13

"**O**KAY, EVERYONE, LISTEN up." Cal raised his hands and turned toward the roomful of people. The campaign suite and two adjacent suites had been flooded by folks from Victoria's campaign manning phones, handling social media, responding to the press, and doing everything in their power to save the campaign. Polling was not good. Victoria had dropped from a six-point lead to statistically even. If the trajectory continued, there was little anyone could do to save her Senate run.

"Victoria ordered dinner and coffee for everyone. It will be served in the suite to our right. Take some time to eat and rest. Tonight will be an all-nighter. While you're eating, the legal team will be reviewing where we are and the information we have. I promise we'll let you know if there is anything we can share."

"Cal, we need to get something out to the press and social media," Paulina said. "After the statements we pushed out this morning, we've been radio silent. That's not good. Any void will be filled with negative information and assumptions."

"We're working as fast as we can and hope to have something to you soon. Now, please, head next door and enjoy your dinner and some time to yourselves."

As the room cleared out, Robert, having returned from police interrogation a few hours ago, and Jenny set chairs around the sofa area where Victoria was sitting. "Is there any hot coffee?" Victoria asked, still groggy. "I don't care how old it is. I just need a shot of caffeine."

"It's cold and about two hours old. I'll make some fresh," Robert offered.

"No need. Just nuke it in the microwave. That'll work for me."

"Okay," Cal began, "I'm sure everyone is aware, but everything we discuss is privileged and cannot be shared with anyone outside of this room." Cal looked at the two investigators and Armond, who all nodded. "Great. Okay, Claire, why don't you tell us what you've found."

"I spoke with Ms. Spanberger's sons. They are devastated, of course. They were both away at prep school and were excited to come home for Thanksgiving—"

"Wait." Victoria held up her hand as she took a sip of her coffee. "You're telling me that a single mom who lived in a bungalow on the South Side of Chicago and worked as ground crew for the airport was sending her sons to boarding school?"

Claire nodded. Victoria threw the blanket off her lap, stood, and began to pace. "How old are these boys?"

"Sixteen. And they were—"

"Not done," Victoria interrupted again. "Just give me short answers. How old was the other boy?"

"Sixteen. Twins," Claire answered.

"Okay, continue." Victoria walked over to the window and looked out at the darkening sky.

"They attend the Thornberry International School in New York. It's pricey and—" She cut off at another hand signal from Victoria.

"Armond, you're from that world. What say you?" Victoria asked.

Knowing Victoria's working mode well, Armond knew her mind was headed somewhere and all anyone could do was work with it. "Good school. One of the top. All male. Typically feeds into Ivy League universities that funnel into Washington, DC, and an internship with Congress or some sort of foreign service position."

Victoria nodded at Claire.

"Okay." Claire now understood from watching Armond that speaking quickly and to the point was the safest route. "The tuition is over seventy thousand per year. You do the math for two boys. Each of her sons is set to participate in an expensive international exchange program next semester. We have, as of yet, found no record of their father. There is no father's name on the boys' birth certificates. They were born at Ann and Robert H. Lurie Children's Hospital in Chicago—one of the best children's hospitals in the country. The mother told the boys and, as far as we can find, anyone who asked that their father died while she was pregnant and that she did not know him well and so has little to add about his family or what he was like. She always refused to give his name when asked."

"What about Spanberger's parents?"

"Thanks to these two"—Claire nodded at the investigators—"we know they are deceased. They were solid middle-class. Mary Ellen's mother also worked as ground crew for the airport. In Chicago, jobs like these are hard to get and are mostly passed down as a legacy from family member to family member. Mary Ellen got her job from her mother. Average salary is seventy-five thousand."

"How much money did Mary Ellen have?" Armond asked, turning to his investigators.

"Average salary, so little savings. But her boys had money," Anthony answered. "We found a trust account with the boys as beneficiaries totaling over fourteen million dollars. We've located no income source that could explain that type of money flowing into a trust for the boys."

"Okay, my turn," Cal jumped in. "Judge Moran is clean. No gambling debts. No mistresses. I know his wife, Katy. He's been with her since before I walked him around the Senate for the meet and greets prior to his confirmation. She's a wonderful woman. He is a devout Catholic and spends a good amount of his free time volunteering around Chicago. They have two children, Kathleen and Joseph, both of whom are in their late twenties. They are a close family."

Victoria snorted.

"The coroner's initial assessment of the cause of death is blunt trauma to the head," Cal continued, choosing to ignore his client for the moment.

Robert pumped his fist in the air, drawing everyone's attention. "I just received a text from the lead investigator. The police have ruled out Victoria and me as prime suspects. They just completed their initial investigation, and since our fingerprints were found only on the outside and nowhere in the home or on the body, they've chosen to, for the moment, they emphasized, move us down their list of suspects."

"That's great news!" Jenny patted Robert on the back.

"Jenny," Victoria interjected, "would you ask Paulina to contact the police and work her magic to get them to release a statement to that effect? That should at least help curb my sinking polls and break our silence."

"Actually," Cal interrupted, "and I know this is going to be hard to swallow, but I prefer that we don't release anything we know just yet. I don't want whoever did this to know where we stand and what we've found."

"We've got no more than twenty-four hours until this story ends, one way or the other," Victoria countered. "Any more time than that and it won't matter who killed her or why they lied about me throwing the jury. Having worked in the political arena your whole career, I assume you understand that."

"I do, Victoria. Remember, I'm on your side. But my gut is rarely wrong, and it is telling me this is the way to go. I don't want to release anything to anyone, not even the rest of the team, until we are ready. Trust me, please."

Silence settled in the room as everyone waited for Victoria's decision. Nodding, she looked at her watch. "Okay. You've got twenty-three hours and fifty minutes. After that, you're fired."

Cal smiled. He could appreciate how difficult it was for someone like her, or him, for that matter, to give control over to someone else. "Got it, and I appreciate your trust, even if it is only for the next—"

"Twenty-three hours and forty-nine minutes," Victoria clipped.

"Okay, everyone, here's where we stand," Cal continued. "Ms. Spanberger's sons were getting money from somewhere, and it sure wasn't from their mother or grandparents. The number one and two questions to answer are where the money came from and why. We'll reconvene in two hours."

CHAPTER
14

THE EARLY SNOWFALL added to the chaos. While it used to be a regular occurrence in Chicago, it had become unusual for it to snow before Thanksgiving. This year was an exception. The snow had begun Friday night at about eleven and continued throughout the next day. The ground had been warm when the snow began to fall, but overnight the temperature had plummeted into the teens, and by the next morning, snow clung to the grass.

"Could you have been any sloppier?" The photos the police released showed a clear path of footprints leading to the back door. "Obviously, they know two people entered the home."

"There wasn't anything we could have done differently. You wanted it done last night. We can't control the weather. But it doesn't matter because we wore covers over our shoes and then destroyed them. There is no link," the first man said as he stood uncomfortably, shifting his weight from one foot to the other.

"Actually, we were lucky," the second man chimed in. "Had we timed it any differently, we would have been in the house when Rodessa and her posse arrived. As it was, we had to wait by the garage until they left before we could leave."

The fire roared in the floor-to-ceiling stone fireplace. The home had been built in the 1890s by craftsmen rumored to have been brought from Italy to lay the stone that was prevalent in its design. This was one of his favorite rooms. It was majestic. He loved and appreciated beauty, whether it was in the form of architecture, nature, or human. As he was doing now, he often conducted meetings by the fire at night, as the room overlooked the blackness of Lake Michigan. While the waves continued to crash against the shoreline for now, in the middle of winter, the waves would freeze midroll, a scene he never tired of. In the summer, the view was equally stunning, as the hand-laid descending stone landings showed off the majesty of the meticulously detailed landscaping that spilled onto a large private beach. The home was secured by the newest technology and gadgets.

A private dock allowed access in and out of the house from the lakeside. Years ago, when Meigs Field had been a functioning airport, guests could fly their private planes directly into the city by landing on the airport's narrow runways that jutted out onto Lake Michigan. His guests were then ferried by one of his boats to his private dock. It had been perfect. No one had known who came or went. He still had no idea why the former Chicago mayor had fucked it up and turned the small airfield into one more wasted space of a preserve.

Shaking his head, he sighed in disgust that he had again allowed his mind to wander off in the middle of a meeting. It seemed to be happening more and more. He was only sixty-five and had so much yet to accomplish. He didn't want to turn into his father—doddering away his remaining years in some shithole retirement community in Florida.

Jesus. Focus. He stood, walked over to the bar, and poured a whiskey for himself. "Where's her body?"

"At the coroner's office. There will be an autopsy," said man number one, as he thought of him.

"Should I be concerned?" he asked in his smooth and calm voice. He had learned from his time in prison that power was understood by action, not words. Everyone who worked with him knew of his past. No one wanted to cross him.

Man number two shook his head.

"Keep it that way. Let me know the minute the coroner's report is out." He turned toward the roaring fire. "See yourselves out."

CHAPTER
15

T WAS TWO in the morning. The cold had not relented. A storm moving in from the west was predicted to dump at least a foot of snow, with winds predicted to hit speeds that had the airlines warning that flights in and out of the city might be canceled. For the past two hours, the wind had been punishing the windows in the hotel suite, feeding on everyone's last nerve as each minute passed. Even the smell of fresh coffee and pastries delivered by room service could not dispel the feeling of dread and despair that hung over the room. They were running out of time.

Armond's phone rang. "Tell me you found something," he almost begged his two investigators. "Are you certain?" Nodding as he listened, he began to smile. "Okay. How fast can you get here? Never mind, I'll pull you in virtually. We don't have time for weather delays. Give me five minutes to gather everyone," he said before hanging up.

"Victoria," he called. He watched as she left her team and walked toward him. Her natural grace and beauty were mesmerizing. He knew they had a lot to repair, but this was not the time. She stopped in front of him and looked up at him expectantly. "My investigators found some interesting information. I'm going to bring them in virtually. Get Cal and your team, and I'll set up the link."

"What is it?"

"I think it best if I only explain this once for the sake of time. But let Cal know it has to do with Spanberger and her mother. I don't know who he will want in the room for it."

"Yes, of course," Victoria said as she walked over to Cal.

Within ten minutes, the suite was cleared of those Cal did not want in the room, and Armond had looped his investigators in through his laptop.

"We found two accounts set up in the names of separate LLCs," Jerome began. "Their ownership is hidden behind a series of complex legal maneuvers, including shell companies. But if we're correct, and we're almost certain we are, both Mary Ellen and her mother received payments deposited randomly into these accounts over the course of their employment at the airport. As far as we can tell, none of these payments were from their employer. In any event, the amounts are not enough to fund the twins' trust, but enough to make life easier for the women."

"How and why would Mary Ellen and her mother receive money in addition to their salaries as ground crew personnel? Who was paying them and for what?" Claire asked.

"We don't have that yet. The financial trail to the source is taking some time to work through."

"Claire, what about on your end?" Armond asked. "What have you found out about Victoria's opponent?"

"Oh, plenty. The dude is a scumbag. He's been married for twenty years, has four children, attends church every Sunday, and has a mistress. She's been in his life for the past ten years. He houses her out of state and takes frequent trips to 'meditate and refresh,'" Claire said, making air quotes with her fingers. "He pays for her on his company's dime, claiming she's his meditation guru and that this is one of his perks as CEO. Really, they've been screwing the whole time."

"Proof?" Cal requested.

"Got it," Claire answered, as she connected her phone to the TV, where explicit photos of Steven Dunne III and his mistress flashed on the screen, leaving no doubt as to their relationship.

"Jeez. I could have done without that," Jenny said, almost gagging.

"Yes, well, when we get out of this, I think the press will be interested in his extracurricular activities," Robert said.

"But who gives a shit?" Jenny asked. "Plenty of people have affairs. It may be morally offensive, but just take a walk down memory lane with our last head of state. How is this connected to whoever set up Victoria?"

"Don't know yet." Cal took a sip of his hot, fresh coffee. "God, that's good." The older he got, the more he appreciated the simple things. "What we do know is that we have loose ends that don't add up. But that means we're getting close. You can't find the answer until you find the question, and we have several. Who were Mary Ellen and her mother receiving money from and for what? Is it somehow connected to the trust for the boys? Does this guy's infidelity"—he nodded at the screen—"have anything to do with this? And, the biggest kahuna of all, why is someone doing this to Victoria?"

Anthony, listening in through Armond's laptop, said, "We have one more question to add to that list. How was Ms. Spanberger involved in this?"

"Okay, everyone, keep digging," Cal said. "Claire, I think you and I need an early-morning meeting with the judge."

"Agreed. But it's Sunday. He won't be in court."

"He'll be there. I requested a meeting for old times' sake, to see if we can clear this up without further acceleration. He agreed to meet at the courthouse first thing this morning."

"I'm feeling a bit helpless. What should I be doing?" Victoria asked.

"You need to be setting up interviews with the press for prime time this evening." Armond walked over and looked into her eyes. They showed exhaustion beyond her years.

"Why would I do that? We don't know what happened yet. That would put us up against the clock—an unnecessary increase in pressure." She shook her head. "The team is under enough stress. I can't add that to the list of things."

"Actually, Armond is right." Jenny came over and laid her hand on Victoria's arm, giving it a squeeze. "Paulina and Tulane have been texting me from the other suite, insisting that we set up a press conference or issue a statement for today's prime time news hour. According to them, we're getting eaten alive on social media and anywhere else people care to give their opinions."

"Okay, fine," Victoria said, relenting. "Armond, would you handle it for me? You've done so many press junkets. Work with my team, though. Keep my avenues open. If we don't yet have anything to say, I'll need filler. I've never been good with BS and don't expect to change by tonight, so please have them prepare some if I need it."

"I will, of course. We'll have it ready and meet well in advance of the deadline to fill you in so you can rehearse whatever lines you might need." Taking her hands in his, he said in a calming tone, "You need to eat something. You've ignored most of the food, and you can't do that. Please. Go take a shower, and I'll bring you some food once you're out. There's nothing more for you to do but keep up your strength."

"Actually, I need to go for a run. But it's the middle of the night, and the weather is not cooperating. I promise I'll eat if you walk with me." Victoria smiled at Armond, knowing how much he hated Chicago winters. Realizing she was almost sniffing the air around him, she abruptly caught herself and pulled back a bit. He always smelled so damn good. She had forgotten. About that and about how he was always in control—or at least appeared to maintain control—even when all hell was breaking loose.

"We have a deal then. We walk in this godforsaken frigid city during a major snowstorm, because that makes sense, and then you'll come inside, shower, and eat. Agreed?"

"Agreed."

<h1 style="text-align:center">CHAPTER
16</h1>

"**C**AL! COME IN, come in. It's good to see you. How long has it been? Twenty, thirty years?"

Cal and Claire stepped into the judge's chambers. The space was impressive. In addition to presiding over the largest courtroom in the building, he had four sprawling inner rooms and an elegant and expansive personal chamber, with separate space for his two law clerks. His courtroom and chambers were on the top floor of the federal building and overlooked Lake Michigan. Apparently, the judge was partial to royal blue, as every room had a touch of that color, albeit in a sophisticated and elegant fashion.

"Judge," Cal acknowledged, shaking his hand. "It's been about as long as you've been on the bench. The last time I saw you, you'd just come out of the Senate hearing. I remember the first thing you said to me was—"

"I remember. 'Whiskey. Now.'" The two men laughed.

"Look at you—chief judge of the Northern District of Illinois. Top dog." Looking around the judge's inner chamber, Cal nodded. "Can't beat this. And the view . . ."

"I'm a lucky man, that's for sure," the judge agreed. "I love my work, my time on the bench, and my family." Then he looked directly into Cal's eyes. "And, Cal, I want you to understand I don't intend to give it up for anyone or anything." The two men stared at each other, and the air changed from one of collegiality to tension.

Clearing her throat, Claire stepped between the two men. "Hi! I'm Claire," she said, holding out her hand and looking up at all six feet of the judge. "I'm Cal's associate. Although I think Cal will tell you I'm more like his partner, particularly since I run much of the show. He's simply forgotten to give me the title, which I'm sure he'll do once we're back in DC."

"Nice to meet you, Claire," the judge said, breaking his stare with Cal. The tension in the room lifted. He signaled to the massive sitting area. "Shall we?"

"Thank you, Judge," Claire began, knowing Cal needed a moment to reset. "We appreciate you coming in on a Sunday to meet with us. I know this is awkward, and I mean no insult, but as you know, we represent Victoria Rodessa regarding the allegations you publicly made about her rigging a verdict."

"I understand. But they aren't allegations."

Claire cocked her head. "Huh. Would you mind if I ask you about that? I mean, how are you certain this is not some wild story made up by a foreperson who, oh, I don't know, pick any of the following: was out for revenge, was bored with her life, or was paid to do it?" Claire opened her laptop, ready to take notes.

"After sitting on the bench for more than twenty-five years, you recognize a liar and a truth teller when you see one. Ms. Spanberger is—or I should say, *was*—a truth teller."

"What, that's it? No offense," Claire clarified quickly when the judge sent her a cold look.

"No. That's not it." Unfolding from his seat, the judge walked over to his desk, picked up a document, and waved it in the air. "Ms. Spanberger was clear in her recollection, and she gave sworn testimony about the events." He tossed the paper gently on the coffee table in front of Claire as he sat back down. "I admit that, at first, I didn't recall the trial. But as she began to tell her story, the details came flooding back. One of the things I remember very clearly is that I was surprised the jury ruled in favor of Ms. Rodessa's clients. In my opinion, the evidence had not gone in well. It makes perfect sense now."

"That's it?" Cal said, echoing Claire's earlier comment. He stood and leaned over the coffee table that separated them. "Why would you believe a woman you don't know but for the fact that she sat in your courtroom as part of a jury? Have you lost your mind?" Cal asked, brows raised. "You went forward with serious and potentially career-ending allegations about a well-respected lawyer and a candidate for the US Senate, and all you have in defense are a few pages of a dead woman's sworn testimony? Are you kidding me?"

"Listen, you son of a bitch." The judge jumped out of his seat, meeting Cal halfway over the table. "I'm no longer the fresh-off-the-farm neophyte waiting for your high and mighty Senate tutelage. I'm the chief judge of one of the most respected federal courts in the country. It seems to me that you are threatening a federal judge, and, as you know, that carries severe penalties. Shall I call my bailiff now to arrest you, or will you see your own way out?"

"Cal," Claire said, holding her hands palms out toward her boss. "We're done here. Let's go."

Walking back to his desk, the judge slid his hand under its edge. The inner chamber door crashed open, and two armed bailiffs ran into the room, guns drawn.

"You've got to be kidding," Cal said, disgusted. "What the hell happened to you?"

"Get them out of here," the judge told the bailiffs. "And, Cal, you'd better be damn certain of where you go with this.

One word from me to the DC bar and you'll be under investigation so fast your head will spin." The judge placed both hands on his desk and leaned forward. "Let me give you some advice. You chose the wrong dog in this hunt. Fire Ms. Rodessa as a client and hightail it back to the hushed corridors you're so accustomed to. You're out of your league in Chicago."

"Are we detaining, Your Honor?" one of the bailiffs asked. The room was still as everyone waited for the judge's answer.

"No. Escort them out of the building. Make sure they don't get anywhere near me again," the judge told them. "The next time one of them tries to enter the building, cuff them and charge them with threatening a sitting judge."

Escorted to the express elevator reserved for sitting judges and their staff, within a few moments, Cal and Claire found themselves unceremoniously tossed out of the Dirksen Federal Building. The snow was falling so hard, it was difficult to see even one city block ahead of them. The wind was gusting, as promised by the winter weather warnings, and there were few people and even fewer cars out and about.

"That went well," Claire shouted into the wind as they tried to take a few steps forward to make their way back to the hotel. "Is that the Midas touch you're always bragging about?"

Shooting Claire a look, Cal grabbed her arm. "Lean into the wind and move it. I see a cab at the next corner, and we need to be in it now, because I've got a feeling it's the last one we'll see until this storm is over."

CHAPTER
17

"HOW'D IT GO?" Victoria asked when Cal and Claire walked into the suite.

While Cal explained what had happened, Claire sat at the table, pulled a document from her bag, and began reading.

"Claire, what the hell are you doing?" Cal asked.

"Reading Spanberger's sworn testimony."

Cal looked incredulous. "You took that out of the judge's chambers?"

"Of course. You were right there when he handed it to me," Claire said, blinking up at him. "Although you were a bit preoccupied with your chest-pounding contest."

"He did not hand it to you. He slid it across the table toward you," Cal argued.

"Well, that was my understanding of the gesture, and since it was directed at me, I get to control the narrative." Claire shrugged. "But form over substance, Cal. You're not going to believe that this is the testimony the judge is relying on. There are no details, no color, no testing of recollection."

"Who was the interrogator?" Cal asked.

Claire looked up at Cal, then flipped back through the document to ensure she was correct before she answered. "The judge."

"Were there any witnesses? Who was the court reporter?"

Claire stood and walked over to hand the document to Cal. "Take a look. No court reporter. The opening indicates that the following was recorded on Judge Moran's phone and then transcribed."

"Let me see it." Victoria took the transcript from Cal's hand and read it while Jenny and Robert looked over her shoulder.

"Victoria," Jenny began, "this is bullshit, no question. He's basing this on testimony that he recorded on his personal phone—no witnesses, no certification by a court reporter, no testing of memory, and no request for corroborating facts. This won't hold up anywhere, especially now that she's dead."

"Agreed," Cal jumped in. "But the problem is that we have only a few hours to bust this open to save Victoria's Senate bid. While we can point out these issues to the press, we cannot rely on the lack of foundation and reliability in the testimony. We must have the end of the story, and we don't have that yet."

"The judge must be involved. I don't know how or why, but he is," Claire pronounced.

"My investigators just called," Armond said then. "They're sending some photos of Spanberger's boys. Take a look," he said, holding up his laptop. "The information on the boys from their school records is consistent with what we've learned. They never met their father, their birth certificates do not list a father's name, and Spanberger never told them anything about him. They know nothing."

Armond continued, "My investigators also got ahold of Spanberger's tax returns, but I'll let them brief everybody on that." Armond called the investigators and put them on speaker. "Hey, Jerome, Anthony, thanks for this information. Give us a rundown."

"Her returns show only the income she received from the airport. None of her other income was reported," Jerome said. "It's interesting, though, because last year the IRS sent her an audit letter, but it was killed within a month after it was issued."

"Okay," Claire interjected, "she likely knew money was being funneled to a trust for her boys. So she must have been working for someone, knew about something, or was covering for someone. Which is it?"

"Whichever it is, I'm betting she knew whatever she was involved in was illegal," Armond said. "And it's likely whoever killed her was either concerned she would tell or decided she'd reached the end of her usefulness."

Cal nodded. "We need to do all we can to find out the identity of the boys' father. That is an overriding unknown. Who knows what answers that knowledge will lead to?" he said. "We also need to know who was paying her by way of the trust for her boys. Then we need to find out who killed her." He looked around the room, meeting everyone's gaze. "And we've got no more than a few hours to get this done."

CHAPTER

18

V ICTORIA WAS TIRED. She had not slept more than a few hours since Friday night, and she knew she had to be at her best for her final interview with Candace, which was set for later that night. If they didn't have the answers they needed by then, she would have to just profess her innocence and hope for the best. But all predictions were that she would lose if they couldn't turn this around.

"Armond, walk?" she asked him.

"Well, it's the middle of a blizzard and about ten degrees if we ignore the windchill. What took you so long for round two?" He smiled at her.

"We'll be back," Victoria mouthed to Jenny, who nodded as she watched them head out the door.

"What happened to them?" Robert asked.

"Oh, you know," Jenny said, waving her hand. "Long distance, travel, work, different life goals, and all the nonsense that can get in the way of a good thing. I still have hope for them, though."

Downstairs, looking out into the cold white and gray, Armond raised his eyebrow and glanced at Victoria in one last attempt to avoid walking out the hotel door.

"Yes, I'm sure," Victoria said in answer to his silent question. "Let's stay away from the lake. It will be windier there."

The wind pushed them along as they walked. It was so strong that they could lean back into it and remain standing. The real hurdle would be when they finally turned to go back toward the hotel. "I know this isn't the most opportune time, but I miss you," Armond said, putting his gloved hand over Victoria's, which rested in the crook of his arm.

She looked up into his eyes and smiled. She missed him more than life. The breakup had not really been her choice—it had been because of her lack of desire for children. "Armond," she began. Then she paused, gathering her thoughts. The last thing she wanted to do was open herself up to more hurt. They had gone over these topics in round after round of discussions—sometimes arguments—getting nowhere. She didn't want to open that door again. Not now. Not when she needed all her energy and emotional strength to fight whoever was trying to ruin her. Knowing she had no choice but to guard what little strength she had left, she said, "I appreciate you coming out to Chicago to help me. But I agree with you, it's not the time."

She glanced up and saw the flash of pain in his eyes before he hid it behind his signature indifference. "Let's turn back, shall we?" was all Armond said.

And with that, they turned toward the hotel, their minds blessedly on fighting the demon wind rather than each other.

ARMOND'S TWO INVESTIGATORS rushed into the hotel suite. "Where's Armond?" Anthony asked the room.

"He and Victoria went out for a bit of fresh air," Claire replied.

"In this?" Jerome looked incredulous. "Well, whatever, we have to find them. We have a development."

Just then, the door opened, bringing with it the cold that still clung to Armond's and Victoria's coats. "What do you have?" Armond asked, seeing the investigators. He went to pour himself some coffee, offering a cup to Victoria, who accepted it just to warm her hands.

"It's the judge."

At that, Cal looked up from his laptop. "What about him?"

"He contacted the boys. He made two separate calls to them over the last few hours."

"What? How do you know?" Claire asked.

Jerome handed Cal the list of phone numbers the judge had called over the past twenty-four hours. Two were circled in red pen. "Here are the boys' phone numbers," Anthony said, handing over a separate sheet listing the boys' names and their two phone numbers, also circled in red.

"Jesus. How did you get a federal judge's number and call log?" Holding up his hand, Cal stopped them from answering. "Nope, never mind. I don't want to know. Is this all verified?"

"It is. There are no mistakes. Our judge has been chatting with Spanberger's kids."

Claire stood, walked over to the TV, and connected her laptop to the monitor. "Well, I think now is as good a time as any to share this," she began. "I called in a favor. I have a friend who works in the genetic and digital AI identification field. Used for all sorts of reasons—to find missing people, to connect children and parents who never knew one another. So I had him run some tests. Look what he found."

Everyone watched the screen in stunned silence as the program ran through facial recognition data at lightning speed, finally stopping at two possibilities. One of which everyone in the room knew.

"Unbelievable!" Cal exclaimed. "I thought I'd seen just about everything. Let's go pay him a visit."

"We can't," Claire reminded him. "But she can." She looked at Victoria. "Here's his home address." Claire handed a piece of paper to Armond. "You should take security," she said. "I suggest you bring my laptop, since it already has the program downloaded. I'll show you how to run it."

Cal nodded his agreement. "The minute you're finished with him, give me a call."

CHAPTER

20

T HE COLD WIND blew against the carefully preserved, century-old lead glass windows as the lake crashed over the retaining wall, slamming wildly onto the lawn. The freezing fingers of water pushed closer and closer to the massive gardens that surrounded the estate, reaching at least ten feet beyond that morning's waterline. *Global warming indeed*, he thought. The weather was colder than ever, and the lake was the highest it had ever been in its recorded history.

Feeling hopeful about the future, he walked into the dining room, where his two men were waiting at the table. "Good morning, gentlemen. Please, eat. Don't wait on me." He picked up a document they had set on the table. "I assume this is the coroner's report?"

"It is. And the most recent police report. They've got nothing. Blunt trauma to the head. No leads."

"What about Ms. Rodessa? I thought her and her lawyer's fingerprints were all over the scene."

"Only on the front door. They've dropped them as suspects."

"Too bad. That would have been a bonus," he said, getting up to throw the reports into the fire.

CHAPTER

21

AFTER PULLING UP to the gated brick mansion on the north side of Chicago, Armond and Victoria sat in the car for a moment, knowing the next thirty minutes would make or break Victoria's run for the Senate and, possibly, each of their careers.

Armond leaned forward to get a better view of the property. "How are we getting beyond that gate?"

"Like this." Victoria pulled her cell phone from her bag. "Cal, we're here. Go ahead." She hung up and waited. In less than a minute, her phone rang. "Yes, Cal. Please connect."

When the connection was made, she said, "This is Victoria Rodessa. I'm outside your home in a black car." She was silent for a moment while Armond stared at her, not believing what he was hearing. "Yes, I understand this is a bit off the normal track. But then, everything about this situation is. I have some information I'd like to share with you, to allow you a chance to respond before I release it to the press." Armond waited while silence again filled the air. "Yes, I think that's best," Victoria said. Then she hung up.

Victoria looked at James, then Armond, before nodding toward the gate as it slowly swung open. A man wearing only a black overcoat walked through the opening. No hat. No gloves. No boots. As soon as she saw him, Victoria turned to James. "We'll want a bit of privacy. Why don't you move into the front with the driver and close the privacy window."

Nodding, James stepped out of the car and held the door open while the man outside bent down to see who was in the car.

"Judge. Good to see you again. Although I must admit the circumstances are not the best. Please, come inside. It's cold," Victoria beckoned.

"Ms. Rodessa," the judge acknowledged, taking a seat inside the car. "Who the hell is this?"

"Ah, this is Armond Renoir," Victoria said. "A dear friend of mine and one of the heads of Renoir Productions. You've heard of them, I'm sure. They've produced some of the most fascinating documentaries over the past decade."

Snorting his boredom, the judge leaned toward Victoria. "Who the hell do you think you're dealing with, Ms. Rodessa? Losing your Senate bid will be the least of your worries. I'm going to have you indicted for jury tampering and threatening to bribe and intimidate a federal judge. Then I'll have you stripped of your law license," the judge threatened. "You've got two minutes. I've called the police, and they'll be arriving soon."

"Not the best move you could have made. But I certainly understand. If I were in your position, I may have done the same. Although, on second thought, I think I would have waited to hear what I had to say." Sweating, Victoria knew she had only a few seconds to cut to the chase. "Well, since you've chosen to cut things short, let me get right to it." Opening the laptop, Victoria popped across to the other seat in the limousine, nearest the judge. "Take a look at this." She turned the screen toward the judge to reveal pictures of Spanberger's boys. She then pushed a few buttons to run the program, as

Claire had taught her before they'd left the hotel, hoping she'd done it correctly. As they watched, a series of barely discernable photos flashed onto the screen at lightning speed, finally stopping on two.

"What the hell is this?" the judge asked, his face flushing red.

"This, Judge, is an amazing new AI digital identification program. It takes photos of individuals and matches their physical characteristics to others in the system. Of course, other information is important, like place of birth, date of birth, and such," Victoria explained. "But for the most part, it can match, at over ninety percent accuracy, the possible genetic relationship of people. It's not failproof, of course, as the matching is done without genetic material. But I'm told it's been incredibly useful for adopted children trying to find their birth parents and in missing person scenarios."

Armond leaned forward. "As you can see, you and your brother are a match to the two Spanberger boys, who are now orphans—or so everyone thought, until you two matched at ninety-five percent."

"I've never seen these boys before. I have no idea who they are," the judge insisted as he reached for the door handle. Outside, the flashing lights of the approaching police cars could be seen cutting through the gray.

"Before you go," Victoria said, putting her hand on his arm, "we know you called the boys after Ms. Spanberger's death. I don't doubt you've never seen the boys before, because you ignored them their whole lives, pretending they didn't exist. But now they have no one. My guess is you just couldn't let them live their lives thinking they were alone."

The judge was silent.

"Judge, you have less than thirty seconds to decide," Victoria prodded. "Either work with us and tell the cops your call was in error, or we tell the cops and the press what we know."

The judge stayed silent as he got out of the car. Victoria and Armond looked at each other, then watched the judge walk toward the police. He showed them his identification, then walked back toward the limousine with one of the officers in tow. Opening the door, he thanked the officer for his trouble and got into the car once again. Sitting in silence for a moment, he looked at them. Then tears filled his eyes. "I've led an impeccable life. Had an unblemished career. One tiny mistake led to this." He sighed deeply. "I'll help you. But I want your help in return."

Victoria rapped on the privacy window. "Let's go. Back to the hotel."

CHAPTER
22

THE JUDGE AGREED to talk, but only with Cal and Claire. Cal insisted, however, that the judge hire his own counsel before they spoke. It took two precious hours before his attorney arrived at the hotel, finished a private meeting with the judge, and reluctantly agreed that he could speak with Cal and Claire.

Victoria was running out of time, and she still did not have the full picture of what had happened and why she had been brought into it.

Finally, Cal and Claire came out of the room.

"Cal?" Victoria inquired, motioning to her watch.

"I'm aware. Let's go next door for a moment."

After shutting the door to the adjoining suite, Victoria sat on the couch and waited. She did not count patience as one of her virtues, so it was all she could do to keep from screaming.

"Here's where we're at," Claire began, laying out the facts they'd just learned from the judge.

When she finished, almost thirty minutes later, Victoria was stunned. One step in the wrong direction and a whole life's work was in ruin, a woman was dead, two boys were left without a mother, and her Senate run and law career hung in the balance.

"How much of this can I share with the press and the public?" she asked. "My live interview with Candace is just a few hours away, and we still need to brief my team. But if I can't share this, then my Senate race is done."

"The judge has agreed you can share it, and he signed an affidavit attesting to these facts, so he can't change his story." Cal slid the document from his folder and handed it to Victoria. "If he does," Cal said, nodding at the document as Victoria read through it, "we'll release his affidavit."

"But who is behind the money?" Victoria asked. "We need their identity to tell the full story."

"That's the rub. The judge wants us to remind you that you agreed to help him. He wants you to go with him to the source," Cal said, a worried look on his face. "He wants you to hear it from the horse's mouth and provide witness to help exonerate him in later proceedings."

"Are you insane?" Armond put his arm around Victoria's shoulders, pulling her toward him. "There's no way I'm letting that happen. She'll likely be walking into a trap."

"I understand how you feel, of course. Unfortunately, it's the only way the judge will reveal the source," Cal said, his palms up. "Otherwise, he said he is afraid for his and his family's safety. The limo is downstairs waiting for you and the judge. Once in the car, the judge will give directions."

"I'm in. Let's get this done," Victoria said, gently moving away from Armond. "I need the full story to tell. I won't be able to convince people to vote for me, or to ever trust me again, for that matter, if everything isn't revealed."

They returned to the adjacent suite, where the judge and his lawyer were waiting. "She's in," Cal told them. "Armond,

Claire, and I, along with extra security, will be close by in separate cars. I expect you to keep her safe."

"What about Candace? She's expecting a live interview," Victoria reminded her team.

"I'll handle her," Jenny said. "If she arrives on time—which I doubt with this weather—she'll need at least half an hour to touch up her makeup. By the time she realizes you're not here, hopefully you'll have the full story."

Victoria turned to Armond and gave him a hug. "Wish me luck."

CHAPTER

23

PULLING OUT FROM under the protective carport of the hotel, their car was immediately surrounded by whipping snow and near white-out conditions. "How long is this going to take?" Victoria asked the judge.

"No more than thirty minutes, forty-five at the most."

"Are you willing to tell me his name?"

"You'll see soon enough."

They rode in silence the rest of the way while the wind rocked their car, eventually turning onto a winding private road lined by mature and well-cared-for oak trees. The car pulled to a stop, waiting for two large gates to slowly swing open. The car continued through the gates and made its way toward the end of a long driveway. Two men came out of the house and reached for the rear car door.

"Judge," one of them acknowledged.

The judge reached out his hand to help Victoria from the car.

"What the hell is she doing here?" one of the men asked.

The judge ignored the question, took Victoria's arm, and led her through the massive front door. "Oh my God," was all Victoria could get out.

"Impressive, isn't it?" the judge said as they walked into one of the most magnificent entryways Victoria had ever seen. The extensive carved woodwork in the curved entryway and the copper inlay in the ceiling appeared original, and the antiquities set behind glass cases throughout the hall were astonishing. Each one was meticulously marked with the era, a brief history, and their country of origin. Victoria doubted if any of them had ever been seen in public. The judge nodded to his left. Victoria followed his gaze to a potato-sized object reflecting light in all directions, slowly turning on its stand. A series of what Victoria assumed were security lights flashed around the case. "The Florentine Diamond. Thought to be lost forever, and yet here it sits. All one hundred thirty-seven carats."

Stunned, Victoria followed the judge as they walked down the seemingly never-ending corridor. *If something goes wrong, I'll never make my way out of here*, she thought. Watching the judge stride so confidently into this home, as if he had been here countless times, Victoria couldn't help but wonder if she'd been set up.

She heard the roar before she saw its source—one of the largest fireplaces she had ever seen, reaching at least ten feet high. Facing the fire, with its back to Victoria and the judge, was a massive carved-wood chair that looked like it could have been a throne from a different time.

"Now, Judge, why in the world would you bring her into my home? Can I assume you've decided to put your family at risk?" A man stood from the chair and turned to face them. With shoulder-length blond hair and unusual peacock-blue eyes, he was one of the most strikingly handsome men Victoria had ever seen. His physique was perfect; there was not one ounce of fat on his body. "Ms. Rodessa," he said, nodding at her, "a pleasure."

Victoria realized she was standing with her mouth open.

"I'm done," the judge began. "She knows. I came to offer you a chance to get out of this mess. I also came because I want to know why you did this. How did you find out about us?"

The man only laughed. "That's bullshit and you know it. You're here because your precious judgeship is at risk and you want to try to salvage it. I've done nothing wrong." The man pointed at the judge. "You're the one who impregnated a foreperson on one of your juries. How do you think the legal community will take to that? I'm guessing impeachment, divorce, and total destruction of your precious reputation. You?"

"How did you get involved in this?" the judge persisted.

"Oh my. I see Mary Ellen never clued you in. A simple story, really, and one as old as time. An unexpected pregnancy created by a married man and a favor come due." The man smirked. "Doris Spanberger, your paramour's mother, was an employee of mine, a valued one at that. She effortlessly fit in with the ground crews and other union workers and would ferret out personal information. Little nasty bits and bobs about her colleagues that I would file away and use when I needed to convince certain union leaders to back off their demands. Of course, she was paid handsomely for her work. Very devoted woman." Pausing, he looked at Victoria. "Forgive my bad manners. Would you like something to drink? A glass of champagne, perhaps?"

Not waiting for her answer, he continued, "So one day, years into our relationship, she came to me with a problem of her own. Apparently, her unmarried daughter had gotten herself knocked up, by a federal judge no less, who wanted her to get an abortion. Imagine this pillar of the Catholic community telling a young woman that he would neither support her nor recognize their child." Glancing at Victoria, the man gestured toward the judge. "Such a shame when a man refuses to step up to the plate, don't you agree?

"In any event," he continued, "a prime opportunity presented itself. I graciously offered to support Doris's grandchildren, who turned out to be twin boys, as you know, and her daughter. I believe you know about their trusts, Ms. Rodessa, as my security reported unauthorized access into these accounts, which I assume was your team. Over the past sixteen years, I've paid significant sums for the boys' benefit. However, nothing is free." He walked to the bar and poured amber liquid into a heavy cut-crystal glass. After taking a sip, he smiled. "One of the finest bourbons you'll find in the States. Ms. Rodessa, Judge, will you join?" He was met with silence. "Ah. I see. Enthralled by my story. I'll continue. As Doris was getting older and nearing the end of her useful life, I agreed to employ Mary Ellen on the same terms as I had her mother and support her boys, making it clear that one day I might want something in return. A special project, so to speak." He took another sip of his bourbon. "Of course, I wasn't certain if that day would come or what that project would be—until Ms. Rodessa decided to run for Senate."

"Why would you care about that?" the judge asked.

"Because," Victoria interjected, glaring at the man by the fire, "Malcolm Wentworth owns the rights to some of the largest oil fields in the United States. And my plan for reducing energy costs and slowing climate change will eventually make his holdings worthless."

Setting down his glass on the side table by his chair, Malcolm gave her a slow clap. "Very good. I'd heard you were smart, and here you are proving it."

"But what does that have to do with me?" the judge pushed.

"Ah. It's quite simple, really. When Mary Ellen and I were done with our business one afternoon, the current Senate campaign came up, as she knows I'm backing Ms. Rodessa's opponent. She happened to mention that she knew Ms. Rodessa indirectly, as she'd once served as the foreperson in a trial for which she was lead counsel." He turned to Victoria. "Quite annoyingly, she extolled your virtues—how well you handled the evidence, how she admired all you had accomplished, on and on." Looking again at the judge, Malcolm explained, "Listening to her talk, though, I suddenly realized I had all the players onstage. The judge who impregnated a foreperson and then ignored his offspring, my employee who owed me a favor, and a woman who, if elected, would be one more cog in the wheel against the oil industry and very likely the deciding vote in the Senate on bills that would destroy some of my most profitable holdings. The only thing missing was their script. So I wrote one, creating the perfect storm. Genius, really." Then he motioned to two other chairs by the fire. "Please, sit. All your standing and staring is making me uncomfortable."

The judge walked over to a large-backed winged chair and sat. Victoria followed and sat in its sister chair.

"I'm at a loss." Victoria looked at the judge. "Did you know you had twins? Were you aware of any of this?"

Shaking his head, he admitted, "Not until about two weeks ago. I received pictures of the boys and a note from Mary Ellen saying she needed to meet with me, that the matter was urgent and concerned my sons." He slumped forward and sighed. "I'm ashamed to say I didn't even know she had gone through with the pregnancy. I certainly had no idea I had twin boys. The last time I had any communication with her was when she told me she was pregnant."

"Tsk, tsk, Judge. Such a low point for a man of impeccable character," Malcolm said, smirking.

Victoria reached for the judge's arm. "Go ahead," she encouraged, afraid this might be her only chance to find out the whole story, as she sensed the judge was rethinking telling his part in it.

"During our meeting, Mary Ellen explained she was being blackmailed by the man who had supported our sons for all these years. She said she now had to pay him back and that involved blackmailing me and ruining you." Looking at Victoria, he shook his head. "She didn't want to do any of this. She truly did admire you, and she didn't want to hurt me. But he threatened the safety of the boys if she didn't follow through. She had no choice. So I had no choice."

"Quite true," Malcolm chimed in. "Continue."

"She explained that she would provide a statement swearing under oath that you had improperly influenced her during the trial. My job was to announce it to the press and make sure it made headlines." The judge winced. "Once your campaign had tanked, everything would return to normal. The trust fund would continue, the boys' father would remain unknown, and I would go back to being a chief judge with an unblemished record and my family intact. If I refused, she would announce to the press that I was the father of the boys, refused my parentage, provided no support, and even asked that she abort," he said, looking at Victoria, his eyes pleading. "I would be ruined, likely impeached, and removed from the bench. The boys would obviously be impacted as well. So, with little choice in the matter, I agreed."

"But when did you learn that he"—she jerked her head toward their host—"was behind it all?"

"Just recently," the judge replied. "I used the only leverage I had. I insisted Mary Ellen tell me who was orchestrating this so I could try to protect both of us and our sons in the future. I convinced her that if someone was this devious, he would not hesitate to request other favors or harm us in the future."

Then the judge looked at Malcolm. "You killed her, didn't you?"

"I didn't personally do so, but yes, I ordered it done," he said, nodding. "She was no longer an asset, and I knew she had not wanted to do any of this. She had a kind heart and never really took to the dirt gathering like her mother had. I had no doubt that someday she would tell someone her story."

The judge rose from his chair, stepping directly between Malcolm and Victoria. "Once she told me who he was, I immediately contacted the FBI."

"You did what?" Malcolm growled, shooting up from his chair. "You stupid son of a bitch!" Reaching inside his jacket, he pulled out a gun. Suddenly the glass along the back wall of the room shattered as shots were fired.

The judge fell to the floor, clutching his left shoulder, blood spilling out at an alarming rate. Victoria crawled on the ground toward him as people rushed into the room. She pulled off her scarf and pushed it against his shoulder. Seeing the judge was conscious, she put his other hand on the scarf. "Keep pressure on the wound."

The room began to spin then, until Victoria found herself also lying on the floor, too dizzy to move. Black dots filled her vision, until everything was dark.

CHAPTER
24

OPENING HER EYES, Victoria saw Armond, Cal, and Claire staring down at her. The room was freezing cold and heavy with the smell of discharged firearms. Nauseous and confused, she lay on the ground next to the judge, who leaned over her, balancing on his good arm. "What the hell are you all staring at?" Victoria snarled. "What happened?"

Armond bent to stop her from trying to stand and gently pulled her to lean back against him. "You've been shot. Superficially it appears, but nonetheless, don't get up just yet."

"Where's Malcolm? He has a gun." Victoria looked around, fearing he was still a threat.

Cal bent down next to her. "Not any longer. See that swarm of federal agents? He's in the middle. The sharpshooter shot the gun out of his hand, unfortunately not before he got off a couple of rounds that hit you and the judge."

Victoria sat up a bit further and felt the nausea subside as one of the paramedics embedded with the SWAT team finished examining her arm. "You're incredibly lucky, miss. The bullet only grazed you. The wound is superficial. I'll clean and bandage it. You're more than welcome to ride with us to the hospital to get a few X-rays as a precaution."

"Thank you. But no. If I feel the need, I'll head to the hospital later." Looking at Cal, Victoria asked, "How did you know when to break in? I knew you were following us, but when did the feds get involved?"

"The judge is the hero here," Armond said, looking at Moran. "He offered to wear a wire so all of it could be recorded, even though he knew that it would put his legacy at risk."

"A wire? What? Why the hell didn't someone think to clue me into this little drama?" Victoria screeched. "I could have been killed."

Cal jumped in. "We didn't know he was wearing a wire until the FBI stopped the three of us and our security detail so that they could position themselves between our cars and yours." Cal looked over at Armond and smiled. "Before the agents had a chance to explain, Armond jumped out of the car, took a swing at one of them, and almost got himself arrested."

Victoria looked up at Armond. "You didn't!"

"I did," Armond admitted, smiling down at her.

"Victoria," the judge said, grimacing as the paramedic continued working on his wound, "I can never repair the damage I've done to you—and, of course, to my boys and their now deceased mother. I am so very sorry."

Victoria inclined her head, saddened by the chain of events that had forever impacted the lives of two young boys, their mother, and a man whom she had admired throughout her career.

"Wait! What time is it?" she asked, glancing at her watch. "Well, you can start repaying me right now. Claire, get Candace on the phone and set up a live interview. Judge, will you appear with me on the interview to clear this up?"

"Done."

CHAPTER

25

T HE WINDOW BEHIND the network's Chicago studio faced Michigan Avenue, and even though it was dark, viewers would be able to see the snow in the background as the winter storm raged on. "Three, two, one." The producer pointed his finger at Candace. Right on cue, her famous smile lit her face.

"Good evening, everyone. This is Candace Sheridan Smith with breaking news. We just received reports about a large police presence surrounding Malcolm Wentworth's estate on the north shore of Chicago. Mr. Wentworth is one of the city's foremost and generous philanthropic businessmen. He runs one of the largest conglomerates in the country." Candace looked over to the side as one of her producers signaled to the large screen in front of her. She nodded. "Just a few moments before I came on air, I was informed that there are eyewitnesses on the scene who asked to speak with me, one of whom is Judge Moran. In full disclosure, I have received no information about the reason for his call or what is happening at the estate. We're hearing whatever he has to say live and together."

One of the cameras focused on the screen where the judge's video call had been cast. "Judge," Candace began, but then she stopped, blinking at the screen, unsure of what she was looking at. "Are you hurt? Is that blood?" she asked after making out a bloodied wrap crisscrossing his shoulder.

"Candace. Thanks for taking my call. And yes. I was shot about forty minutes ago, and so was Ms. Rodessa. She's here with me as well." The judge moved the phone camera so it could pick up Victoria, who was sitting next to him on the floor, shoulder to shoulder, leaning back against one of the ornate sofas.

For one of the first times in her life, Candace was at a loss for words. Hearing her producer snap his fingers, she recovered quickly. "I see. Would one of you like to tell our viewers what is going on?"

Victoria nodded for the judge to begin. "I very recently learned that I have twin sixteen-year-old sons. Not knowing about them was my fault. I spoke with them for the first time hours ago." He paused as tears unexpectedly filled his eyes, the events of the last few hours catching up with him, as he realized his family would be learning the truth along with the rest of America.

Knowing the judge needed a moment, Victoria picked up the thread. "The judge was blackmailed by Ms. Spanberger, the mother of the twins and the foreperson who accused me of tampering with a jury."

"Let me, Victoria. I've got this," the judge said, taking back the phone. "Candace, for now, it's important that your viewers and the voters of Illinois know that Ms. Rodessa did not tamper with a jury, nor did she improperly communicate with any juror, including Ms. Spanberger. Ms. Rodessa is one of the finest lawyers who has ever appeared in front of me. While more details will come out later, for now, your viewers should know that because of her policies on clean energy, she was a threat to some powerful individuals." Turning to look at Victoria, he continued, "Ms. Rodessa was a victim in all of this. I will do all in my power to make it up to her and to the people of Illinois. For now, though," he said, smiling, "I fully endorse Victoria Rodessa as the next senator from Illinois."

Before Candace could ask her next question, the screen showed the ceiling, and someone could be heard saying, "We've got to get him to the hospital now. He's lost too much blood." The phone connection was cut.

26

CHEERS WENT UP at Victoria's campaign headquarters. The national news networks had just called the election and announced Victoria as the next senator from Illinois. The room was packed with Victoria's team and her most dedicated volunteers. The campaign's theme song began to build, and the champagne flowed. Johnnie was in his element onstage, whipping up the crowd and getting them ready to welcome their candidate as the new senator from Illinois.

Paulina and Tulane stood beside Victoria offstage, giddy with excitement, having successfully handled their first campaign after their time in the West Wing. "Congratulations, you two!" Victoria hugged each of them. "I could not have done this without you. You have incredible futures ahead of you."

"We couldn't agree more," Tulane said, smiling and nodding at Paulina. "We survived allegations of jury tampering, a rogue federal judge, a murder, and the shooting of our candidate. Not bad for our first run after the West Wing."

"Thank you, Victoria." Paulina grasped Victoria's hands. "You not only trusted us with your campaign but also showed us how true leaders work in the face of real adversity. If you ever want to run again, maybe for a certain White House, let us know."

"As Ms. Rodessa's personal counsel," Jenny interrupted, smiling as she walked up to the group, "I'll have to advise her to take the Fifth about any future plans." Glancing at her phone, she said, "I just received the final numbers from the secretary of state. We finished an incredible ten points ahead of our opponent. What a comeback! Now, I suggest we all get out with the crowd, celebrate, and let our new senator get ready to meet her constituents," she said, ushering the group away and following behind them.

"I just got off the phone with Cal and Claire," Armond said as he joined Victoria. "They heard the news and wanted me to tell you how happy they are and that they look forward to hosting you in Washington."

Turning to look up at Armond, Victoria smiled. "I'm so incredibly proud of you," Armond continued as he took her lightly by the shoulders and kissed her forehead. "Go get 'em, V!"

"Thanks, Armond." She turned and laughed as she saw her cue of red, white, and blue confetti begin to fall. Shaking her head at Johnnie, she started to walk onstage. Then, turning back to Armond, she asked, "How do you feel about living in the capitol for half the year?"

"I thought you'd never ask."

Keep reading for an excerpt of

DEVIANT AGENDAS

Book 1 of the V-Files

Where it all began…

CHAPTER

1

THE DAY WAS one of those picture-perfect Chicago days; few and far between, but unbeatable when they happened. The weather was warm and sunny, with just enough of a breeze to rustle the oak trees lining Lake Michigan's shoreline. Victoria took a deep breath as she scanned the growing crowd. Pride and contentment fought with the adrenaline racing through her veins. Moving to the side, Victoria lifted her gown and hopped on a riser so she could have a shot at finding her best friend in the sea of people.

Finally! Victoria thought. After three grueling years, she had only to get through this ceremony to become a graduate of The University of Chicago Law School. After being mentally poked and prodded by professors, spending exhausting hours up all night learning about the "eggshell plaintiff," constitutional rights, and the rule against perpetuity (some archaic rule that governed property law, which Victoria planned to never use, let alone utter, once she passed the bar), she and her peers had finally earned the right to be called "counselor," "lawyer," or "advisor."

While typically Victoria had little use for pomp and circumstance, today, she simply smiled with appreciation. For forever, the University had been hot on the heels of Harvard and Yale, always falling somewhere in the top five, yet never taking the number one or two spots. But for the first time, the predictions from those in the know were that this year's ceremony would push Chicago into the number one spot because the President of the United States, one of its most famous former professors, was to deliver the commencement address. The demand for tickets had been greater than ever, the crowd larger, security tighter and the press, everywhere. Victoria could almost taste the excitement. Good juju was in the air.

Still searching the crowd, Victoria saw the dean nod to the band, and the music began. The first few rows of Victoria's classmates had already taken their seats. As rehearsed, the rest of her peers began to meander toward their seats, knowing they had the luxury of one more song until the ceremony officially began. Victoria stretched her small frame higher one last time to find Kat.

Glancing toward the front, Victoria saw Chad move to his seat on the podium, and had to smile. He looked like he was about to puke. Unlike the other one hundred eighty students sporting maroon and gold tassels, Victoria and Chad had bright blue and yellow tassels hanging from their caps signifying their near-perfect marks. Chad had beaten Victoria by a few tenths of a point, and so would give the valedictory speech.

Victoria was actually thankful that Chad had received the honor. She wanted to enjoy the day and not worry about delivering a perfect and moving speech, especially since the President was speaking immediately after Chad.

"V! Over here." Kat waved as she moved through the crowd toward Victoria. As soon as she was in reach, she squealed and grabbed Victoria in a tight hug lifting her off the riser and twirling Victoria's petite frame around in sheer delight.

Kat smiled as she let Victoria's feet hit the ground. She was struck as always by Victoria's natural beauty. Wavy, chestnut hair, long and thick as a horse's tail but soft as butter, spilled out of the careless knot in which Victoria usually wore her hair and her beautifully proportioned face glowed with excitement.

Reaching inside her graduation gown, Kat pulled out two splits of perfectly chilled Roederer Cristal champagne. She handed both bottles to Victoria to hold while she expertly popped one, then the other, open. Victoria smiled as she felt the chill of the bottles loving the fact that Kat would never think to offer champagne, even bottles hidden away inside her commencement robe, at other than the perfect temperature.

"Congratulations, V, we did it! No more slogging through four-hour exams or staying up until all hours of the night reading boring case law! We're done! I can't wait to get off this campus and into the real world." Holding her bottle in the air, Kat toasted, "To real jobs! That pay real money!"

Victoria clinked her split with Kat's and smiled. "Cheers! To us! To the end of three years of nonstop reading, debating, writing and memorizing. To the end of totally useless pieces of information that are forever stuck in my brain! To no longer being battered and abused by professors practicing the Socratic Method simply because they can and are pissed at the world!"

After drinking from the bottle, Victoria cocked her head and offered the toast that held real meaning for her. "To the beginning of power. The kind that almost knocks you to your knees when it walks into the room. To our lives with that kind of power."

"*Salút,*" answered Kat. And the two young women at the beginning of their professional lives happily chugged the remaining champagne just as the musicians concluded the "sit your asses in your place" song.

"This is it!" Flashing one of her full-kilowatt smiles, Kat pulled Victoria into a tight hug, gave her a smacking kiss on the cheek, and ran back to her spot near the front of the line.

"Don't forget to meet me after the ceremony by the basilica!" Victoria yelled to Kat's retreating back.

Victoria smiled as she watched Kat work her way back to the front. Kat had it made. She was going to work for her family's real estate business and had been groomed to do just that from an early age. She had grown up following her father around on different construction sites. All the photos of Kat and her father Victoria had seen during their time in school, had shown the two of them with matching hard hats at some construction project. In each picture, Kat wore the same expression. Determination. Whether her focus was school, men or work, it all received the same lazer-like attention. Kat, Victoria thought, with a purpose and in full pursuit, was a thing of beauty.

Victoria took her seat and tried to pay attention to the dean's opening remarks. Looking into the stands, she found Sophia watching her from her first-row seat. Smiling, her mother blew a kiss and patted her heart. Something she had done for as long as Victoria could remember. Raising her hand to wave, Victoria thought of how good it would feel to finally be able to pay her own bills and no longer be a drain on her mother's income.

The applause began as the President of the United States and other dignitaries took the stage, snapping Victoria out of her semi-daydreaming, and now a bit-buzzed state. After what seemed like forever, the speeches finally over, the first three lines of students rose from their seats and walked toward the stage, ready to receive the bit of paper that signified the beginning of their new lives. In two days' time, Victoria thought, she would begin her next life chapter at the law firm everyone said was destined to become one of the most important and powerful firms in the world. There was no doubt in Victoria's mind that it was exactly where she belonged.